Vegas STORM

D.M. DAVIS

ABOUT THIS BOOK

D.M. Davis' **Vegas Storm** is a spicy, billionaire, recovering bad boy, contemporary romance of mistaken identity, misconceptions, and rules that were made to be broken.

There are two things you should know about me: I don't gamble. I don't date.

Relationships are not my thing.
I have fully vetted, no strings attached *arrangements*.
No repeats.

Then I kiss the wrong woman.
Mix up my *arrangement* with a business deal.
That's a line I never intended on crossing.
Yet, I can't stop thinking about doing it again.

There are exceptions to every rule.
I pride myself on not being one of those exceptions.
She prides herself on proving me wrong.

I'm willing to gamble my future for a chance with her. Only, she calls my bluff.

Never gamble what you're not willing to lose.

DEDICATION

For all the guys who forget they're lovable.
And for the women who remind them they are.

Vegas STORM

Chapter ONE

STEPPING INTO THE RESORT'S KITCHEN, THE smell of fresh bread assaults my senses, and for a split second I forget where I am. I'm just a boy in Midtown helping my father in his New York bakery. Hot bread, muffins, pastries, bagels, cakes, every mouthwatering baked good I could ever want within reach. I'm still the faithful son who believed in the wonders of the world, a father who was king to our family, a mother who gave the best hugs that left me smelling like vanilla and roses… Where the worst part of my day was getting my shoes wet, and the best part of my day was jumping in the puddle that drenched said shoes.

Simple.

Innocent.

Naïve.

I eye the cheese Danishes on the cooling rack. If I snag just one, surely Father won't notice.

"Mr. Storm?"

I blink, and the sense memory fades. The bustling kitchen in my Vegas Tower Resort and Casino comes into view. That fresh-baked bread has my mouth watering for a taste.

"Dmitri." The brusque use of my given name has me turning to face Felipe, my head chef. "How are you, sir?"

"Hungry." I slip my hands in my pants pockets, eyeing him and then the food preparation going on around me, wondering if my breakfast is somewhere getting cold. "My food never arrived."

I could have called, but I find handling it in person tends to get the message across more effectively than a brisk phone call. Showing up once usually means no further calls.

Felipe turns beet red. "My apologies, sir. Our system—"

I hold up my hand. "I know." I sigh at the reminder of our software issues. "I don't need apologies. I need food."

"I will prepare it myself and have it sent right up, Mr. Storm." No Dmitri this time? How quickly he slips from employee to friend and back.

I don't make a habit of friending employees. Felipe is an exception. He and I go way back to when we were boys running the New York blocks like we had the world at our fingertips. Like we had any idea what that meant. Our world was small, safe… until it wasn't.

On a quick nod of thanks, I leave him to deal with his staff as I wrangle my morning to heel on an empty stomach.

Zeke falls in line as I head to the elevator. The distant hum of the casino seeps in through the back corridors, free of prying eyes and unwanted attention.

As we step inside, he swipes his keycard to grant us access to my penthouse suite before facing me. "I could have handled that."

He's in a foul mood this morning.

I hide my smirk at his grumpiness. "It's done." It's a simple fact, yet it rubs him the wrong way.

As head of my personal security and bodyguard, food is one of the few menial tasks Zeke doesn't usually deal with. While I will admit to occasionally sending him out for tacos or other late-night indulgences after a long day, I try to keep the lines of responsibility clear, and dealing with my diet doesn't fall under his realm of duties.

"Any word from Stefan?" My brother tends to play harder than he works. And by *work*, I mean, he shows up every now and again, shuffles papers on his desk, sends a few emails, hires and fires an average of two people a month, and then breaks for a five-hour lunch consisting of vodka, cigars, and women—not necessarily in that order.

I put up with it.

He's blood.

He's family.

My penance as the oldest. My responsibility since our parents were killed.

"I'm working from here today. Let Max know, will you?" I step out, leaving Zeke to do what he does.

"Your *therapy* is at eleven." His face doesn't crack. There's no hint of judgment or concern.

"Even more reason to work from home." The doors close behind me as I head to my home office. I glance through the back windows to the patio, considering going for a swim before my breakfast arrives.

Maybe after therapy when I'm relaxed and able to enjoy it.

"Ms. Vaughn, you may go up now." Mr. Storm's assistant directs me to a different elevator than the one I entered from the lobby. She swipes a card in the elevator and steps out. "He's working from home today."

I nod, wondering if I'm the reason. He doesn't need to be here for me to do my job, and anyone could have let me in.

Honestly, I probably could have done this remotely, but the person who called my assistant insisted I come in person.

So, here I am.

I run my hands down my skirt, checking my makeup in the dark-mirrored elevator walls. Should I have worn slacks? His assistant is wearing slacks. I sigh. It's too late now. I just hope I don't need to get on my hands and knees.

I should have worn slacks.

The elevator dings, sliding open to a bank of windows overlooking the Vegas skyline. I stutter a step, taking in the view. I bet it's even more impressive at night.

A deep voice draws me to the entrance of the massive living space with more windows. In fact, every wall I see is a window.

How does he get any sleep—or privacy—with all this glass?

I glance up and gasp at the sheer height of this place. His *home* has to be three stories atop The Tower Resort and Casino. To the left are stairs leading up *and* down. Could it be four stories?

He must have done something right to have all this. Maybe he could teach me a thing or two. I'm doing fine, way better than I was a few years ago. But I'm nowhere near *multi-story-penthouse-living* fine.

"Ahem."

I swivel, gaze locking on the striking man in a dark gray suit at the other end of the room. His dark hair is neatly coiffed, jaw set with confidence with one hand in his pocket, the other holding a phone to his ear as he rakes me from head to toe and back, sticking on my face, appraising. One eyebrow rises.

What is he thinking?

Does he find me lacking?

Does it matter if he does?

I stiffen my spine, stepping forward to introduce myself—

"Last door on your left." He motions down the hall then gives me his back.

Dismissed.

He *dismissed* me.

Son of a…

He's a job, not a prospective husband, I remind myself as I head down the direction he deemed me worthy to go. *I don't have to like him to take his money.* I know that's entirely too true. Asshole money spends just as well as anyone else's.

I get to the end of the hall and step through the *last door on the left,* seeking equipment, only it's a bedroom. *His* bedroom by the size and pure masculinity of it. Everything is dark, except for the one drawn curtain that lets in some light from the outside world. Dark coverings are spread out on the dark wood bed, its massive headboard decorated with intricate details I squint at but can't discern in this low light, flanked by dark end tables. Even the plush furniture in the sitting area is dark. The walls and carpet are gray—maybe silver; it's hard to tell.

Dark. Dark. Dark.

Dark as his soul? I'm beginning to believe so.

Though, what I'm really trying to figure out is why I'm in his bedroom? What I need can't possibly be in here.

"Sorry to keep you waiting." His voice glides up my spine, notably gentler, nearly sensual and entirely too close.

I turn, backing away, giving me space to breathe, to assess, to—

He tosses his jacket on the back of a chair as he steps forward. His gaze is more than assessing, nearing flammable as he removes his tie. "Are you shy, Skarbie?"

Scarb-yeh? I frown, taking another step back as he presses forward.

Why is he unbuttoning his shirt? Wow, okay, that's not a body you see every day.

He stops, so close. His tantalizing scent has me fighting the urge to lean in, bury my nose in his neck.

Our bodies nearly touching, he scans my face like a caress. "Hmm?"

I nearly forgot he asked a question: *Am I shy?* "No." The breathiness of my voice is embarrassing and hardly vouches for the truth in my words.

What's happening?

"No?" He cups my cheek, running his thumb along my bottom lip.

Is he going to kiss me? My heart pounds, as I wouldn't mind that at all.

He leans in. His minty breath mixes with his already panty-dropping, make-me-moan, I-am-man scent, making it impossible to think, to breathe, to remember why I'm here.

He presses his mouth to mine. I suck in air, gasping. My eyes widen in shock, and I freeze in place for *more* until his hot lips move over mine, and I… kiss him back.

"Skarbie," he whispers into our kiss.

Scarb-yeh, I repeat in my head as if it means anything to me. It must mean something to him as he's said it twice now. He has no accent except when he says *that* word with a roll of the r, making it sound dirty, inviting, and foreign. The lilt of the word sounds French or Italian, but with a more Russian sound. None of which I speak. Apparently, he does—one of them, I'm fairly certain.

His tongue brushes mine, tenderly coaxing, and I moan, gripping his shoulders, meaning to push him away in the name of professionalism, but end up pulling him closer. His answering groan has me tingling and contracting in places this man—a complete stranger—shouldn't be anywhere near.

Tell that to my rubbery legs.

"Let me," he mumbles between sucking my bottom lip and my tongue. At some point, his hold on my cheek traveled and now sinks further into my hair as his other hand slides up my side, slowly kneading, caressing my breast, stopping to brush over my hard nipple before tweaking it, drawing another gasp from my lips. Deftly, his fingers graze across my other breast, only now his warm touch is under my blouse, over my bra and bare skin.

What am I doing? Sentient thought breaches my lusty stupor. I tear my mouth from his and step back, panting like I've just run miles on my treadmill—which I haven't done in a long while.

He frowns, reaching for me.

I sidestep him, backing away from his hands. "What are you doing?"

"I would think that's obvious. I'm trying to undress you since you weren't naked as instructed." The bite of his tone pushes me farther away.

"Naked as instructed?!" Horrified, between his words and the sight of my blouse unbuttoned to my navel, I continue to edge backwards, pulling my shirt closed to cover myself. "Who do you think you are?"

He crosses his arms, making his muscles bulge. He's tall and lean, but there's no missing the strength of his form. "Dmitri Storm." Agile like a cat, he closes the distance between us, gripping my hip, pulling me against his hard body, and damn it if I don't sink into him a little despite myself.

"But you knew that, didn't you?" He squeezes my ass, grinding me against his erection, his eyes dark and feral. "I don't do seduction." He kisses the corner of my mouth then my neck. I suppress a groan. "But for you, Skarbie, I could make an exception."

I fight my baser need to stay and experience his form of seduction as my body is inexplicably turned on by this man I don't even know. I push his chest. "No."

His features tighten as his eyes narrow. "What game are you playing?" He steps back.

I take a full breath, shaking my head, finding my sense, and take advantage of the space—I run down the hall toward the elevator, pressing the button over and over.

He rounds the corner, need and anger rippling along his body.

"Stop!" I hold out my hand, not taking my eyes off him.

He pauses, then scowls and presses forward.

"Please! Stop." The elevator opens, and I step inside. "I'll call the police!"

He moves but doesn't step over the threshold, his hands braced on either side of the elevator's frame. "What?"

"Whoever you think I am. Whatever you think I'm here for." I sweep my hand between us. "I promise you, it's not this."

His biceps clench, fighting the urge to join me or rip me from the elevator and use whatever skills he has to persuade me to stay.

His eyes don't waver from mine as the doors close, sadly barricading me from him.

Chapter TWO

WHAT THE ACTUAL FUCK? WHAT IS SHE playing at?

I call Max.

"Mr. St—"

"Who did you send up?" I'm curt and short on time if I'm going to catch my little Skarbie.

"Oh, um… Ms. Vaughn."

"Who the hell is Ms. Vaughn with?" I rush to my room.

"Casandra Vaughn," she says it like it should be perfectly clear.

I grab my shirt and dash to the elevator, sending a text to Zeke with Ms. Vaughn's description and orders to stop her before she leaves—in the nicest way possible. Hopefully, she valeted her car and didn't hop into a taxi waiting at the curb.

When I don't respond, because I'm texting with Zeke, Max adds, "From Vaughn Tech. You asked to meet with her personally and not send a lackey to work on our system issues."

My stomach sinks. "*Kurwa!*" What have I done? "Thank you." I hang up and call Zeke as the elevator descends, buttoning my shirt.

"I have her. East Valet." He hangs up, knowing I don't need more than that.

If he can convince her to step inside, he'll take her somewhere private. But I have a feeling Ms. Vaughn is not open to being swayed by any more strange men today.

When the doors open to the lively sounds of the casino and those mulling around the hotel lobby, I've just finished tucking in my shirt and rolling the sleeves. Not my normal look for business. But this is turning into an abnormal day.

Shaking off the edge of unsatisfied desire, I make for the east entrance.

I immediately spot her just beyond the exterior doors, her curly, light brown, shoulder-length hair swaying in the breeze. Her scowl cannot diminish her beauty. She's a fucking diamond among a city of rubies and sapphires. She eyes Zeke speculatively, arms crossed, foot tapping, not taking any shit from him. He has a look of indifference, but I know he's fully tuned into her mood and actions and those around him.

He sees me first and backs up. When her eyes land on me, her scowl deepens and her cheeks flush. I ache to touch her silky skin and supple curves. Instead, I focus on her blush, stepping close. Closer than I normally would with a woman I haven't even officially met but have kissed and touched intimately. The dragon in my pants stirs to be reacquainted with her dizzying attraction.

"Ms. Vaughn." I motion inside, hesitating to touch her lower back, driving her in the direction I wish her to go to ask for another chance at a first impression. I hold off, quite sure I've pushed her beyond her limits. "A moment, please."

"I need to go." She eyes Zeke. "He won't let me leave. Like *I'm* a criminal."

I gently touch the back of her arm, needing the contact, the reassurance, damn it, to see if that magnetism is still there.

"I promise, this is not how he treats criminals. You're practically family with how close he's standing to you." I tip my head.

Her eyes soften as she fights a smile.

"Please, have a drink with me. Let me… explain."

How, exactly, am I going to explain I mistook her for an escort?

I widen my smile, clear the doubt from my eyes and pray she'll give me a moment of her time.

"One drink," she agrees, moving out of my hold. "I don't need you manhandling me. I can walk beside you without your assistance."

That fire. So different from the meek woman I mistook her for a few minutes ago. I thought she was shy. Perhaps she was only surprised, taken off-guard. Whatever she was—she was turned on, panting for me to do all those things I envisioned in my head the moment she stepped out of the elevator and into my home.

I intend on getting her back there sooner than later.

Business, not pleasure.

"Of course." I motion forward. "This way, please." I run my hand down my nonexistent tie, wishing I'd taken that extra second to grab it and my jacket. My suit is my armor, and I'm certain I'll need it to survive the woman beside me unscathed.

I let out a punch of air as I press my palm to my heated cheeks, dropping my hand when Mr. Storm side-eyes me with that darn quirking brow of his before quickly looking away. Silently, we walk side by side through the hotel lobby, through the casino, and stop at the lounge beside the poker tables. The place is surprisingly busy for this time of day.

I *never* hang out at casinos—anymore. I avoid them like the plague, except when work requires me to forget my moral compass in favor of a paycheck.

"Do you play?" Mr. Storm looks from me to the beautifully kept professional poker tables corded off and surrounded by official-looking men and women guarding the gate to Eden.

"No." I smooth out my skirt, ignoring the call, the thudding of my heart to… "Could we go somewhere else?" You know, somewhere not surrounded by the *beeps* and *chimes* of slots machines, the shuffle of hundreds of decks of cards, and the *clang, clang, clang* of coins—the sounds of shattered dreams and wasted meal tickets?

He frowns but nods. "Certainly." He motions for me to follow as he pulls out his phone, texting someone before sliding it back into his pocket.

Despite me asking him not to, his hand lands on my lower back, and instead of stepping away, I relish the warmth of his touch, letting it calm my racing heart and addled thoughts.

I anticipated him taking me to one of his award-winning bars like Marquee or Tranquility, yet I'm surprisingly relieved to find ourselves in the homey atmosphere of Storm Grill. The hostess enthusiastically greets us—well, *him*. I'm apparently invisible.

After we're shown to a private circular booth in the back, he waits for me to sit before sliding in next to me, forcing me to slide over or sit with him pressed to my side. Not a terrible idea on the surface. But a horrible idea when I remember I need his business not his *business*.

He places his hand on the back of the seat, near my shoulder as if he's as tempted to touch me as much as I'm tempted to let him. Yet his assessing gaze is on the server as she approaches, not me. Her hips sway nearly as much as the hostess' who sat us.

"Good afternoon, Mr. Storm." Her smile is sweet and a little too eager. "I'm Candi, and I'm honored to serve you."

Candi? That can't be her real name. I feel wrinkled and lacking next to her youthful pink radiance—and I'm still in my twenties!

"Hmm." His grumbled response pulls my eyes to him as his finger toys with a wisp of my tousled curls before his eyes slide to mine. "We've just gotten in some new wines I'd love for you to try."

"I'd rather have a scotch." If I'm going to drink, let's make it count.

His lips tip at the corners before dropping to face the woman begging for his attention. "Two Macallans, neat."

The server spouts something entirely too enthusiastic before trotting off. His attention on me, he hardly notices. Points for him.

The seconds tick by as my heart pounds in my ears. His gray assessing eyes eat me up like I'm his main course—or perhaps anticipated dessert. I don't dare look away, feeling like I'll fail some test if I do. His eyes crinkle as he blinks, his hand lowering from the back of the booth, brushing my arm. Purposely or accidentally, sparks surge through me, reminding me of his intimate touches. My skin prickles as heat rises to my cheeks.

He frowns. "I am sorry for earlier. If I'd known who—"

"Who did you think I was?" Does he typically kiss and undress women he's only just met?

He clears his throat. "I'd rather not say."

Candi sets our drinks down, eyes on him. "Are you ready to order?"

Are we eating? I agreed to a drink, not food, but my rumbling stomach doesn't care. I pick up the menu, searching for something, anything, to not have him waiting on me.

"Is there anything you don't like?" He pulls me from my speed-reading perusal.

"Peas and Brussels sprouts," flies out of my mouth before I consider I sound like a petulant child.

A smirk pulls at his lips. "My sister is the chef here. Would you mind if I order—"

I wave him on, relieved. "Knock yourself out."

He glances as Candi. "Ask Mina to surprise us. Nothing crazy. No peas, Brussels sprouts, or beets."

"Yes, sir." She slips away as quickly as she came.

I relax now that he offered up a food he doesn't care for. "Beets?"

He shudders. "Can't stand them."

"That's how I feel about peas." Now that I think about it, the list in my head of foods I don't particularly care for grows, but I keep it to myself. I can just pick out anything I don't want. I'm an adult. I no longer have to eat what is set in front of me.

He chuckles. "Noted." He takes a sip of his scotch, his eyes never leaving mine. Setting down his glass, he slowly licks his lips before offering, "I have a proposition I'd like to discuss."

Chapter
THREE

I CAN'T KEEP MY EYES OFF HER. EVERYTHING about her screams to my baser needs to *claim* her, *keep* her. And I've never wanted to keep anyone—*ever*.

But maybe…

"What kind of proposition?" Her face squishes like she just bit into a sour candy.

She needs more time. "Have dinner with me on Friday, and we can discuss."

Her eyes narrow as she studies me, trying to figure out my game. "We're having lunch *now*. Why can't we discuss it now?"

"Because I want you to say *yes*."

She laughs. "And you don't think I'll say *yes*?"

I take a slow sip of scotch, welcoming its smooth burn. "I'm certain you won't."

"You want to bet on that?"

"Ms. Vaugh—"

"Casandra or Cas, please."

I nod, taking it as a good sign she doesn't want to remain formal. "Casandra, despite the fact that I own a casino, I only bet on sure things."

"Oh, you're one of *those*."

"One of what?" I tip my glass, gazing at the caramel liquor as if it's more fascinating than the woman before me. It's not.

"The type of gambler who walks away when they're ahead."

"No, Skarbie. I'm a man who walks away before my money even hits the table. I don't bet. Ever."

"Shame. I bet you have a killer poker face." She downs her drink in one gulp, then holds it up to the passing server, asking for another.

We eat up the silence as I finish my drink, watching, wondering what she'll say next.

She leans forward, her nails clicking against her empty glass. "Do you know why I was here today?"

I do now. "You're here to fix your software problem." I can't hide my dissatisfaction in her product.

Her brows fly up. "*My* software problem?"

"Yes, it's *your* software."

She shakes her head. "No, Mr. Storm—"

"Dmitri or Dima," I insist, though it's probably not smart to interrupt, given her frustration over her system issues.

She lets out a huff of air. "It's not *my* software. I put in a bid for the job six months ago. You didn't hire my company. I didn't even receive a courtesy *thank you but no thank you* call or email from Storm Enterprises to let me know you'd gone with the other contractor."

What? How did we get it wrong? I was positive I approved Vaughn Tech for the job. I may not have recognized her name when Max said it earlier, but now it's sinking in who she is and why she's here today.

Definitely not an escort.

She leans in closer. "*You* went with a subpar company who installed a flawed system because you liked their low-ball bid. Now, when it's not working, and they're nowhere to be found to fix *their* system, I get a phone call from some guy demanding I be here this morning to meet with you in person, not send a flunky—which I don't have any, by the way. And what do I get?"

I flinch, knowing what's coming.

"Mauled," she seethes, her eyes boring holes into mine. "I get mauled by you, followed by your security guy, and now, when I don't comply, I'm asked what type of game I'm playing?" Rounding the other side, she slides out of the booth. "Thanks for the drink, Mr. Storm. Good luck with *your* system."

She shoots out of the restaurant before I can catch up to her. She's fast in those heels. Just outside the entrance, I grip her elbow to slow her roll. "Casandra, please. Wait."

She rounds on me, anger rolling off her in waves.

"I'm so—"

"You're sorry?" She shakes her head. "You've said that a lot today, and we've just met."

I scrub my face with my hand and think of another tactic. "You're right, but it doesn't mean I'm not." I've never apologized this much to anyone.

She looks around, patting her skirt before her face softens into embarrassment. With a deep sigh she admits, "I believe I left my bag in your penthouse."

I thank the stars for the reprieve. "Come back inside, enjoy our lunch. I'll have Zeke bring your bag. Unless you'd like to go back up—"

"No." She walks past me toward the restaurant entrance. "That won't be necessary. Your Pitbull can bring it."

My Pitbull? Zeke will love that.

I'm many things, but patient is not one of them, unless I'm coding, working out a computer problem, or focusing on numbers—any equation or formula will do. That's my holy grail.

Running my business, interacting with people, putting up with bullshit is far down on my patience scale as Mr. Storm just found out.

Fresh drinks, appetizers, and a basket of hot rolls welcome us back to the table. As he did last time, he waits for me to slide in before joining me. I don't know if I didn't move over enough, but he feels closer than before.

Grabbing a roll to quell my hunger pains, I admit, "I'm a little hot-headed when it comes to being misunderstood or underappreciated. I'm sorry I walked out on you. I completely understand if you no longer wish to work with me." I slather butter on the hot center, squishing it back together before taking a rather unceremonious bite. I groan as the tangy sourdough mixed with the salty butter hits my tongue. "Dang, that's…"

"Heaven," he offers, buttering one for himself, a small smile rimming his mouth.

"Yes. Absolutely heavenly," I agree.

"It's my grandfather's recipe and starter." He's rather reminiscent about it.

"Warm bread is my downfall."

"Mine too." He hands me the buttered roll I thought he was making for himself. "I'll have some packaged up for you to take home."

"Th-thanks." He's being kind, and I was a total asshole to him. "I really am sorry."

He shakes it off. "You can thank me by helping me with my

software issues. I'm sorry about how all of that played out. I'd like if we could work together from here. Fresh start."

I offer him my hand to shake on it. His brow quirks, but he seizes it, giving it a firm grip. "I'd still like to take you to dinner on Friday."

Removing my hand from his, I consider his offer, wondering what his proposal is and warning myself not to jump too far ahead of ourselves. "Let me take a look at your system, see what's going on, fix your problems. Afterward, you can see if you're still interested."

"Oh, I'll be interested." The innuendo in his tone sends a shiver up my spine, making me squirm in anticipation of a touch that never comes.

"I don't know. You may be too broke to afford to go out."

He laughs. "Then we'll stay in, and I'll cook."

"You cook?"

"Don't look so surprised. My parents had a bakery. Me, my brother and sister, we all cook. If we didn't want to eat bread and pastries all the time, we had to learn to cook our own meals. Running a New York bakery was a twenty-four-seven job for them."

"I can imagine. I'm not much of a morning person. I prefer the nights."

His smile grows. "I'll keep that in mind when I'm making your breakfast."

I nearly choke on my water. He pats my back, still smiling like a… "Cocky much?"

He touches the back of my hand with the tips of his fingers in a slow circle. "Not cocky. Confident in what I want."

I fight the urge to giggle like a teenager. "And what's that?"

Slowly, he leans in, brushing his lips across my jaw before planting a kiss on my cheek. "You, naked in my bed."

Repressing a moan, I take a slow breath, calming my girly

parts from flagging him in. "It's not a good idea to mix business and pleasure."

His thumb barely ghosts the edge of my bottom lip as he watches the movement before locking on my eyes. "I tend to agree. But in your case, I'm finding that line entirely too easy to cross."

"Which could mean we shouldn't."

His eyes darken. "Or it could mean we should."

Chapter
FOUR

DESPITE MY CLAIMS THAT I'D BE PERFECTLY happy to work from a conference room, an empty desk, or a broom closet near the rest of his office staff, Dmitri insisted I use the private conference room attached to his office. Not that I mind working in the lap of luxury. I mean, how much did this chair cost anyway? It's like sitting on a cloud. Not to mention the footrest Max brought me while I was setting up my laptop. Oh, and two large monitors Zeke set before me as his team worked on my system access. I didn't mention the fact I could have accessed the required systems or data without the clearance.

It's probably best not to hack a new client on the first day just because I can.

It only took a few hours to flush out the system software issues. A few tweaks here and there, and it was running smoothly again. For now. The holes I found in his cyber security are what need his immediate attention. He didn't hire me for cyber security, but I'm beginning to believe he needs to. In fact, his entire system needs an overhaul.

After four hours, I've completed the fixes that should temporarily hold, laid out a time table for the additional changes that need to occur, and the cost and precedence for each phase. I've also provided a knife-edge approach: the delivery of a completely new system from the ground up all at one time. It's the best option from a system perspective—cleaner, but far harder on the employees' learning curve and job satisfaction.

"You're frowning."

I look up to find Dmitri leaning against the doorway between his office and the conference room, hands in his pockets, a smirk sitting casually on his lips. His sleeves are still rolled up, showing off his muscular forearms, making a girl think thoughts she shouldn't.

I lean back, take a breath and watch as he stalks closer with the confidence of a man who takes charge in every room he finds himself in. Taking the seat next to me, he pivots to face me, not even glancing at the monitors or the papers strewn across the table. "I've hardly seen you look up since you started working. Is it that bad?"

"You've been watching?"

He points to the cameras in the corner of the room behind me and in the opposite corner with a shrug. No apology for the privacy invasion.

It's not like I didn't know. I was in his system—every clean and dirty corner of it. I saw the cameras, the video feeds. I don't mind him watching. I have nothing to hide. "Surely you've got better things to do than watch me work." He has employees for that. I wonder if they paid close enough attention to notice I was observing them too.

"I wouldn't say *better*, but definitely pressing matters that pulled me away from watching you get lost in—" he motions to the papers and the monitors, "—all this."

"You want the good news or the bad news?"

He groans, then nods to the door as Max enters with a tray of food, followed by another woman with even more food and drinks. "You haven't eaten, barely even took restroom breaks. I figured we could eat while you broke the news."

"Grilled cheese?" I nearly melt at the sight.

His smile is indulgent. "Not just any grilled cheese. It's with my family's sourdough bread, white and yellow cheddar, gruyere, and parmesan cheese."

"You had me at sourdough." I stand, taking a second to stretch before moving toward the plates of food. Not just grilled cheese but hamburgers, omelets, a charcuterie board. "It's amazing."

"Go on." He hands me a plate with half of the grilled cheese before taking the other half for himself, turning to lean against the table. "Don't let it get cold."

That first crunchy, buttery morsel followed by oozing cheese is pure decadence in my mouth. My eyes fly open at the sound of him taking his first bite. "Amazing," I murmur around my mouthful.

He scans my face, his gaze heating as I lick breadcrumbs from my lips. "There's nothing like it, Skarbie."

"What does that mean?"

"Hmm." He takes another bite, piles food on his plate and saunters back to his seat. "Someday I'll tell you. But not today."

I decide to let it go, assuming it's not a derogatory term by the gleam in his eyes when he says it. I just met the man, but there's something about him that speaks to me beyond his power, confidence, and sexual magnetism. Any one of them on their own is tempting enough, but given all three, it's a heady combination.

"You have viruses." I set my plate down and grab us some waters and napkins. "Lots of viruses… like deadly computer cholera viruses."

He frowns mid-chew, waiting for me to continue.

"Lucky for you, I'm the CDC of virus control. I wiped them

out and set measures to keep them out. But you need to limit employee access to highly prone sites of contamination."

"You're my disease control agent?" He smirks like I'm amusing, but his possessive *my* makes my heart skip a beat.

What would it be like to be his?

"Yes, I'm Casandra the Disease Control Agent, CDCA." Maybe I should put that on my business card.

"Got it. What else?"

"You've been hacked."

"Hacked?!" His alarm is understandable.

"Numerous times. But it wasn't to steal data. It was more to mess with your systems—to cause system blips, failures—small, but you've obviously noticed them, or I wouldn't be here." I finish my half of the grilled cheese and start on half of the omelet.

"Is there more?"

"Afraid so."

I slide over my suggested upgrades. "You need a complete overhaul." I point to the incremental plan. "You can piecemeal it and stretch out the pain, or you can bite the bullet and do a knife edge cutover, fully tested beforehand, of course."

"Okay." He nods. "What else?"

"How do you know there's more?"

"Because the glee is still dancing in your eyes like a kid in a candy store. You might be delivering bad news to me, but you're excited for having slain my dragon."

Why does that sound so dirty and feel so good?

Shocked he noticed my elation, I swallow around my food, chasing it with water. I love chasing dragons. The bigger they are, the harder they fall.

I slide over another piece of paper, tapping it. "You need a forensic accountant. Stat."

"What am I looking at?" He eyes the page then dismisses it, wanting the details from me.

"Someone is skimming money off these accounts. I need to look into it further, but it's occurred too regularly for it to be unintentional. I can find whose access is being used, but I'm not an accountant. I do love numbers, but I don't have the credentials you'll need for this." And a part of me wonders if I'd have been better off not knowing.

His eyes narrow as he studies my face long enough to make me nervous. "Why were you looking into my accounts?"

"It's what I do. I'm a bloodhound. You gave me a scent, and I followed it to every nook and cranny of your system. The obvious issues were a mere distraction from what was really going on. I think it's all connected, but when we start talking money, transfers, and financial institutions—I'm out. It's not my cuppa." Not my wheelhouse, not my expertise.

I power down my laptop. "The name of the guy I recommend is at the bottom of my invoice. You don't have to take my word—in fact, I hope you don't. Get a second—third opinion. Whoever did this tried to cover their tracks, but they aren't as smooth as they think they are."

Slipping my laptop into my case, I stand. "I didn't charge you for that part, by the way." I slide over my invoice for today's work. "I can keep looking to find out everything I can about who's doing it, or I can drop it and consider our business done. It's up to you."

I leave him stewing. It's a shock. He hired me to fix his system issues. I did that.

Job done.

Chapter
FIVE

AFTER CASANDRA LEFT, I SAT THERE RAGING at my own stupidity and misplaced trust, getting angrier and angrier as I read over her invoice and started scanning the printouts she'd left behind. My gaze was drawn to the chair she sat in most of the afternoon and well into the evening time and time again.

She exceeded my expectations.

Intelligence written all over her, keen eye, wit, and sharp words.

I let her walk away for a reason.

This is business.

Yet I already admitted it's a line I have no trouble traversing for her.

I send her a quick text, thankful I acquired her cell number before she started working on my system.

Me: *Keep digging.*

I call Zeke to my office as I gather the papers she left and ask Max to schedule a meeting in two days' time with the forensic accountant Casandra recommended. But I'll have him vetted before he sees a single account file. I let Casandra in perhaps a little too easily, and I let my dick rule my brain. The minx didn't just come inside, respectfully slipping off her shoes. She stripped bare and danced in my fields and devoured my sheep, but damn if her tenacity doesn't turn me the fuck on.

When my text goes unanswered and doesn't show as read, I send a follow-up, though the text status doesn't necessarily mean she hasn't read it. She's technical-minded. She could have turned that feature off.

Me: *I was an ass. Sorry.*

I felt raw, seeing the deceit done right under my nose, to *my* company, and I had no clue. She may have pried further than I would have liked, but if she's right, can I really complain she found a weakness I can now eliminate?

Mój Skarb: *I'll let you know what I find.*

Short and concise. No flirtation or acknowledgment of my apology. Perhaps she needs time to forgive.

Maybe she's just busy.

Maybe I've overwhelmed her with the whiplash of our first encounter, our tumultuous lunch, and the revelations that high-lighted my flaws.

Me: *I'd still like to take you to dinner Friday.*

This time dots bounce as she replies.

Mój Skarb: *I don't think that's a great idea.*

This is not looking good. If she won't agree to dinner, she certainly won't agree to my proposition.

Me: *It's a great idea. You can't deny we have chemistry.*

Mój Skarb: *Bleach and Pine-Sol have chemistry, but they produce a toxic gas. Not all chemistry is good or healthy.*

Should I be this turned on by her brain? She just compared me to a toxic gas. I shrug.

Me: *I've been called worse.*

Mój Skarb: *Are you always this positive?*

Me: *I'm positive I'm attracted to you.*

Mój Skarb: *It's just your hypothalamus releasing the neurotransmitter dopamine, making you feel happy.*

It's not happiness causing my cock to swell uncomfortably in my pants.

Me: *Another chemical reaction?*

Mój Skarb: *So to speak, yes*

Me: *Have dinner with me. I promise not to dopamine all over you.*

Mój Skarb: *LOL. That's not quite how it works.*

Me: *You can sexy-brain talk me through it over dinner.*

Mój Skarb: *I'll think about it.*

She didn't say *no*. I'll take it.

If she's purposefully playing hard to get to make me want her more… it's working.

When did I start flirting with clients? Oh, that's right. Never! I'm an idiot for how I handled my first encounter with Mr. Storm. I let him kiss me—*grope* me under my blouse. I'm not a shining star of professionalism at the moment. It was entirely too easy for him to draw me in, causing my brain to overload with hormonal need. It's *ridiculous* how easy it was.

Apparently, I'm in need of carnal attention, but getting that from Dmitri is not a smart move.

"You look like you can use this." My brother Gavin hands me an ice-cold beer. "Don't balk at it. Not everyone can afford your taste in scotch. Besides, if you gave IPA beers half a chance, I think you'd come to appreciate them."

Not likely.

Scarlet bounds from down the hall, snagging my beer. "Thanks." She sticks her tongue out at Gavin, plopping down next to me on the couch. "You weren't really going to drink this, right?"

I shrug. I was tempted to, but being the brat she is, she saved me from sinking to the depths of desperation to start drinking the foamy bitterness. "I've had more than enough scotch today."

Gavin scowls between us. "Drinking on the job now, Cas?"

"You worked all day?" Scarlet talks over our brother.

"Yep. I met with Mr. Storm, remember?"

"Oh, shit." Gavin sits up, fully invested in the rundown. "I totally forgot."

"How'd it go? Is he as hot as I hear?" Scarlet would have slept with Dmitri. No qualms about it and absolutely no guilt. She accepts herself. That might also be one of the key reasons she's not the face of my company despite how charismatic she is. She's a rockstar with computers—we all are—and she *rocks* her sexuality, but it doesn't mean I'm okay with her sleeping with clients. Not because she's whoring herself to get jobs—she'd do it because she wants to, and her libido trumps common sense at times—most times when it comes to feeding her *kitty*.

I don't call it that. *She* does.

The idea of her sleeping with *this* particular client prickles inside me ridiculously.

Quickly deciding which details to withhold, I fill them in on my meeting with Mr. Storm.

Gavin tips back his beer, finishing it off before grabbing my sister's empty on his way to the kitchen, shooting over his shoulder, "You slept with him then?"

"What? No!" My flaming cheeks aren't missed by Scarlet, who simply raises her brows in surprise but doesn't say anything. I shake her off, hoping she'll stay silent about my blush. But she narrows her eyes. "I didn't. Swear."

"Hmm." Gavin returns with a water for me and two more beers for them. "Something happened."

"He asked me out." Maybe a little of the truth will suffice.

"Is that where the drinking came in?"

"No, that was lunch."

"I'm confused." Gavin holds up his finger as if he's going to draw a diagram in the air. "Your appointment was for eleven. So instead of getting to work, you had a drinking lunch with him and then got to work fixing his system, thusly discovering he'd not only been hacked, but you uncovered an embezzlement scheme as well?"

"Pretty much."

"When did he ask you out?" Scarlet is being absolutely no help, redirecting back to the sex.

"Over lunch and just now via text."

"He's texting you at ten o'clock at night?" Gavin grouses, his head hitting the back of the couch. "So much for that contract."

"Hey, he told me to keep digging. He's planning on using us."

"Oh, I have no doubt he's planning on *using us*." Gavin air-quotes. "And by *us* I mean *you*."

"I didn't say *yes*," I defend.

"It doesn't really matter. He's got it in his head he wants you. We'll lose the job either way."

"How do you figure?" Scarlet narrows her eyes on him.

"He'll feel jilted, denied, if she says *no*. And if she says *yes*, he's soon to be disappointed."

"Hey!" I throw a decorative pillow at him, hitting him in the face.

Bullseye! Take that!

"No offense, Cas. But you haven't been on a date, much less slept with anyone in ages. You probably have cobwebs up in there." He waves in the general vicinity of my lap.

Scarlet laughs a little too loudly and snorts, making herself laugh harder.

"That's not funny. And it's not true." I felt anything but cobwebby up in there when Dmitri was kissing me… and those hands. Goosebumps erupt along my arms, flames lick at my dreadfully ignored desires, fanning them awake.

Gavin scoffs, "It is true—"

"It's like riding a bike—"

"That's true," Scarlet agrees. "If she was ever any good in bed—it will come back to her quickly."

"Hey!" I push her off the couch. "You know I *let* you two live here. I could easily kick you out." I grab my water and phone and stomp out of the room, giving them my back and my silent nasty rebuttals.

What do they know?

I'm not bad in bed.

I'm not.

"You love us too much to do that," Gavin's yell and their hyena laughs follow me all the way to my room.

"I could fire you too!" I own the company, after all.

That only makes them laugh harder.

On an eye roll and a smirk, I slam my door and get ready for bed. I definitely don't give Mr. Tall Dark and Sexy another thought.

Nope. Not a single one.

Chapter
SIX

COFFEE IS THE MANNA OF LIFE. AT LEAST ON this morning where I'm dragging from a restless night and awoke with a hard-on the size of a torpedo, which aches for a troublesome *skarb* no matter how many times I release the tension.

I don't do relationships. I don't date. I don't pick up random woman. Hence the reason for my weekly *therapy* sessions where the women fit my standards and are thoroughly vetted. They know the score. And scoring me as a boyfriend or anything beyond a one-time fuck is never going to happen.

It's in the contract.

Foolproof.

Except when my team gets the women on my schedule crossed, and I end up trying to nail the *kobieta* who merely came to resolve my system issues, not my cock-needs-sucking issues.

The aforementioned cock sated for the moment, I slick the water from my hair. I dry off and get ready for breakfast with my siblings. Though, who knows if Stefan will even show.

Coffee first. It's my credo and will probably be on my tombstone.

The deep, dark roast fills my senses as I step out of the

bathroom. Max comes up early to start my coffee most mornings. If she doesn't, Zeke will do it. It's a good thing as it's been years since I've had to work a coffee machine. Not that I can't. I learned young in my father's bakery. Made coffee and breakfast for my younger brother and sister until they were able to chip in and eventually take over the more domestic duties as I focused on making a living once our parents were gone.

I can make my own damn coffee. I just don't have to.

One rule we kept as we grew, graduated from school, and became adults was eating breakfast together at least a few times a week. With our busy schedules—my sister and me—it can be hard to do, but surprisingly it's not the two of us flaking out. It's our brother who can't seem to find his ass in the morning to make his way out of whoever's bed he found himself in the night before.

As I near the kitchen, the scent of bacon mixes with the coffee, which can only mean Mina is here and started on breakfast.

"Good morning, *siostrzyczko*." I kiss her hair on the way to the coffee pot.

"Little sister," she sighs under her breath. "Will you ever stop calling me that?"

I pour a cup, noticing she already has one. "No." I smirk at her rebuff. She'll always be my *siostrzyczka* no matter how old we are. "Any word from Stefan?"

Her low grumble lets me know she hasn't heard from him, and she's not too pleased about it. "The last time I saw him, he was all over Cindy. I'll never forgive him for using my friend to slake his need for random hookups."

"If he knows her, then it's not all that random, is it?"

Exasperated, she glares at me. "You know what I mean. She's. My. Friend."

It's poor form on his part, agreed, unless he truly cares, which I doubt is the case. Knowing Stefan, he was thinking of his dick and not Cindy. "I'll speak to him." When I see him, which, by his absence, won't be today.

"Don't bother. He won't listen. He does what he wants, when he wants, and with whom he wants."

My fuck-up from yesterday comes to mind—mistaking Casandra for a… "We can't all be as perfect as you."

"I don't need or expect perfect. Considerate. That's all I'm asking."

"I'll still speak to him." I squeeze her hand before grabbing our plates. "Let's eat and talk of more pleasant things."

"Like root canals?"

I bark a laugh that stops short when I see her face. "You're serious?"

"Unfortunately," she grumbles. "It's tomorrow. Can you pick me up?"

"I'll *take* you."

She motions toward me. "See. *That* is how a brother is supposed to behave. Not try to screw his way through my friends."

I blanch. "He's done this before."

She sighs, "Yeah. Too many times."

"Maybe you need new friends?" I mean, he's a cad, but he's not a monster. He only pursues willing partners. They could say no.

"Maybe I need a new brother."

Fact. I fork a bite of my Denver omelet. "Maybe."

"Not you, though. You're the *best-est* brother."

"I'm your *responsible* brother. That doesn't make me the best-est."

"It does in my books. You put me through culinary school. Gave me a restaurant—"

"I gave you an opportunity. You excelled all on your own."

"Still—"

I point at her plate. "Eat. I'm not interested in sainthood."

She laughs. "No, you're still an ass half the time. I think saints have to be ninety percent asshole-free."

"It's settled then." I pat my chest. "Decent brother. Horrible saint."

"I'll agree to that."

I'm surprisingly satisfied with the turn of events. I prefer my sister's company over my brother's most times. He's too confrontational. Always competing for things that aren't a competition. I'm the oldest. I'm better at most things because I've been around longer. I've had more experience, and I didn't have the luxury of not succeeding. Failure meant we didn't survive our parents' deaths; we didn't stay together; I didn't keep a roof over our heads, food on the table. Failure was—is—not an option. But that doesn't mean he can't be successful in his own right. He just has to try. He has to want to succeed more than he fears failing. Most of all… don't give up.

Stefan doesn't give up because he doesn't even try.

The rest of breakfast is spent talking about business and plans to open another restaurant catering to the afterhours crowd looking for a greasy meal—aka hangover cure—after a night of clubbing.

"Morning, Max." I smile at the steaming cup of coffee on my desk. The slogan on the side is facing the door, so I can read it as I near my desk:

The house always wins.
But I own the house.

It's the truth of the statement that makes me laugh and the fact that I would never choose a slogan mug for myself. It's cheesy AF, but funny.

I rarely arrive at the same time each day. I don't know how Max knows when to pour a cup just in time for it to still be the perfect temperature to drink immediately. She has a sixth sense about these things. *Or* maybe she has a tracker on me. Both are possibilities. I wouldn't put either past her.

"Ms. Vaughn called this morning. I told her you didn't have any openings to meet with her today. She said she'd email you."

I don't like the idea of Max putting her off, but I do have a full day. Also, why didn't Casandra call my cell directly?

Lines.

She's trying to keep the lines between business and pleasure in place.

The more she draws, the more I want to step over them.

But not obstinately—because, surprisingly, I want more of her.

I dig into my email, putting the woman out of mind long enough to get some work done. That is, until her email comes through.

Chapter
SEVEN

I'M ACTUALLY RELIEVED DMITRI WASN'T available to talk or meet today. I need distance from his overpowering masculinity. He oozes sexual confidence like it's the air he breathes. There's no creep factor. It's pure, unadulterated *I know what you need* and *I crave giving it to you* confidence that makes my knees quake and my panties wet.

Maybe my brother is right. It has been far too long since I've *dated*.

I run my own company. I live, eat, and breathe work. I don't have time to date. I'm not interested in meaningless hookups. Which means, if a potential partner doesn't work for me or he's not a client, there's little chance of me actually meeting him out in the wild. And neither employees nor clients are a viable dating pool.

I'm tempted to agree to a date with Dmitri.

I've never been tempted before.

This is new territory.

I'm on the fence.

I need distance.

I relish my busy day working on a new custom system for one of my first clients, who gave me a chance fresh out of college.

I had an abundance of confidence and no self-editing skills to *only* deliver a handful of things done well. I busted my ass trying to do *all things*, all on my own. Thankfully, I had my brother and sister, who were just starting out, ready to jump into the job market, and each had the skillsets I needed.

Gavin is full of direction and drive. He can preemptively spot a challenge and the most lucrative solution. He excels at staying on task, ensuring all decisions support the end goal.

Scarlet is abundantly creative and lives so far outside the box, she doesn't even know there is a box, nor does she care. She's not restricted by boundaries or *shoulds*. She takes no prisoners and never asks for forgiveness. Because she's *not* sorry. When the path is clear, it's a given in her world that's the way we should go. Her crayon box has three billion colors, and the human eye can only see approximately one million. She's on another level.

When lunch comes and goes without a morsel of food passing my lips, it's nearly five o'clock before I stalk to the kitchen looking for something to snack on. Finding the refrigerator sparse and the cabinets even sparser, I resort to salivating over takeout menus, daydreaming of ordering from all of them, knowing that's an extravagance I can't afford fiscally or physically.

"Cas." My assistant finds me devouring a smushed package of Club Crackers that's seen better days. She blinks at me before continuing, "Mr. Storm is on line one for you."

I choke and cough cracker-crumb shrapnel, patting my chest in an attempt to ease my breathing and compose myself. Wiping my face and the front of my clothes, I rush to my desk and chug half a bottled water before picking up his call.

"Mr. Storm, how can I help you?" I cringe at my attempt at a cool façade. I'm undone by the thought of talking to him.

"Step outside, and I'll tell you." The timbre in his voice does naughty things to my insides.

"What?" I glance out my window to find Dmitri leaning

against a black sedan. He's wearing sunglasses so I can't see his eyes, but I swear he's staring right at me, and my body temperature rises exponentially.

"Bring your purse, your laptop. You won't be coming back."

"Like, ever, or tonight?" For some reason, I'm not markedly opposed to either option.

He smirks but doesn't let the laugh free I can feel in his stance and the bow of his head. "Five minutes or I'll collect you myself." He hangs up, sliding his phone into his pocket.

Dmitri coming in to collect me is more enticing than it should be. Heart racing, I turn my back on him and start to collect my things, grumbling, "Mr. Bossy Pants. Who is he to demand I leave my own place of business? What if I have an appointment? Or a date."

"Do you?"

I scream and jump back, clutching my phone to my chest, scowling at Mr. Tall, Dark and Bossy Pants leaning against my door frame. "Don't sneak up on me."

He straightens, hands in his pockets, and steps into my office. "You didn't answer me."

"I have lots of things I need to do. But, no, I don't have an appointment." *Lucky me. I'm free to be all yours.* What was it I was saying earlier about needing distance? This is not it. I tuck my laptop into my case and glare at him.

"And do you have a date?" His jaw clenches as if he doesn't like the thought.

"I could. Someone asked me out just yesterday." I tip my chin in defiance as I grab my purse and bag and sidestep him, heading for the exit, thankful most of my staff is busy or have already left for the day.

He quickly catches up, taking my bag. "Was that someone me?"

Arrogant much?

It was, in fact, him. But he doesn't need to know that.

I exit the front door and turn left.

A strong hand grips my elbow, halting my progress. "We're right here."

"No. *You're* right there." I point in the direction of the building's parking lot. "*I'm* parked back here."

"I'll bring you back for your car." He tries to steer me toward his car waiting at the curb, his driver holding the back door open expectantly.

"I'd rather not come back to a dark empty parking lot. Tell me where we're going. I'll meet you there."

When he only narrows his eyes at me before typing a message on his phone, I turn, pulling out of his grasp, and head for my car. Honestly, I could just go home. I wasn't lying when I said I have lots of work to do. There are never enough hours in the day. Not complaining. It's a great problem to have.

After unlocking my car, I slip inside, setting my purse and bag on the floorboard behind the passenger seat. I shut my door and reach to hit the lock button. A second before the lock engages, Dmitri opens the passenger door and slides inside, giving me a side smile with an exasperated exhale as he grabs his seatbelt. "Do you do *anything* the easy way?"

"And by *easy*, you mean *your* way?"

"Exactly." As if his way is the only way.

"If you're looking for compliance, I suggest you buy yourself a woman whom you pay not to think for herself." I point beyond the windshield. "I hear there are tons of escort services with women just dying to make you happy."

Stunned, he blinks a few times before he finds his bark. "Why would you say that?"

"Because you have a shit ton of money and can probably buy anything or anyone you like—"

"You?"

I laugh, putting the car in reverse. "Except me." I pull out of the parking lot and ease to the curb where his car is sitting. "I don't need your business bad enough, Mr. Storm, to put up with your arrogant, egotistical opinion of women." I unlock the door. "I'll courier over my final report tomorrow. I highly suggest you hire a forensic accountant. You're going to need one."

"You're kicking me out?"

"I'm ending our business relationship, wishing you well, and, yes—I'm kicking you out. There's only room for one dick in this car, and that's me. You're messing with the quota."

Calm, cool and collected, he steps out of the car, bending down, drumming his fingers on the roof, locking eyes with me. "Since you no longer work for me. You're free to have dinner with me Friday night."

This guy. Does he ever give up? "Actually, because I no longer work for you, I'm free to *not* have dinner with you Friday night. Goodbye, Mr. Storm. Have a nice life." I screech away, forcing him to step back or get run over. The passenger door slams shut from the force of my departure, echoing through the car like the last spark of my love life flickering out.

Chapter EIGHT

WHAT IS IT ABOUT THIS WOMAN THAT makes me stupid? After she drives off, I stand, mouth gaping for a second—which is a second entirely too long, before I climb in the back of my car and direct Sergio to take me home.

I'm not even pissed she kicked me out. I was being an ass. The fact that she called me on it is not nearly as surprising as the fact I'm rock hard for her. Her balls of steel turn me the fuck on.

Her dick line is the highlight of my day, maybe my year.

There's only room for one dick in this car, and that's me.

But her firing me as a client won't do. I need *mój skarb* working for me, with me, and most definitely in my bed—under me, riding me—as often as possible. I should settle for one or the other, but I want both. I'm not sure which I want more.

Bed. It has to be in my bed more than saving my company. Maybe.

Did I only meet her yesterday?

How is that possible?

I've kissed her, nearly devoured her. I've felt the softness of her skin, her lush curves, felt the beating of her heart, and seen the lace of her bra with her hard peaks taunting me. I've felt her breasts, tweaked her nipples, and heard her sighs of arousal.

I've angered her twice now… Maybe three times if you count the kissing and chasing as she fled my penthouse.

We've shared two meals.

She's delved into my books, had access to things few do.

She's pissed *me* off three times: when she ran the first time after we kissed; the second time during lunch; and just now, when I had to chase her—again—to her car because she couldn't just be agreeable and come with me.

It's like she has a point to prove: she doesn't need me. She doesn't need anyone. She's highly intelligent and quick to spark.

She's goddamn combustible.

And I can't. Get. Enough.

In my penthouse, I pace in front of the wall-to-wall windows overlooking the Vegas strip. My skin is too tight. I'll go crazy if I stay here, doing nothing, and let her walk away so easily. If she's going to walk away, let me at least taste heaven before ripping it from my arms.

I call my sister, getting her voicemail immediately. I check the time. She's getting ready to hit the first wave of the dinner rush when families typically want to eat. The singles, dates, childless couples wave will come later. It's not as cut and dry in Vegas, particularly when patrons are coming in before or after hitting a show. But families with younger kids rarely detour from earlier dinners.

I sigh in relief when my phone rings. "Mina, thanks for calling me back."

"What's up?"

"What do you get a woman who needs so much but won't take a damn thing from you?"

She laughs and waits. "Oh shit. You're serious."

"Yeah." I run my fingers through my hair, discarding my jacket on the closest couch.

"Is this about Casandra Vaughn?"

My hackles rise. I don't even like my sister knowing shit about me unless it comes *from* me. "How do you know that name?"

"How do you think, silly? Max told me she ruffled your feathers."

That's the understatement of the century. "You could say that."

"She's not biting?"

"Oh, she bites alright."

"Eww. Hush. I didn't need to know that."

"I don't mean—"

"It's fine. The only thing…" She's silent for a moment, but I don't say anything. I can practically hear her brain ticking along. She snaps. "Oh, I got it! Your time. Your perseverance. Your heart."

I scoff, "I don't have one of those."

"Sure you do. You've just forgotten how to use it. It's that thing behind your left chest plate that goes thump, thump, thump."

"Funny." My sister the comedian. "I can do the other two, though."

"You should try the heart thing, Dima. You deserve to be loved and to love."

"I love you and Stefan, though I try not to most times."

"Haha. Now who's being funny?" She covers the phone, hollering an order. "I have to go. My boss is a real *kurwa'*."

"Watch it," I growl, playing right into the role of cantankerous boss.

"I love you. Please consider the love angle. I need a sister. Someone to shop with and take my side against you and Stefan."

"My woman would take my side." *My woman*? WTF?

She laughs. "Not if she's right for you, she won't. She'd have a mind of her own, which won't always agree with you."

Sounds like *mój skarb*. "Have a good night."

"You too."

I hang up and eye the bar across the room. Without thinking on it too long, I stride over, grab what I need and head out.

"Food's here!" Scarlet yells from her room as if I didn't hear the buzzer.

"I'll get the plates." Gavin sets our drinks on the counter before opening the cabinet.

I wish he'd use paper. It's easier clean up, and the last thing I want tonight is to do dishes. "I guess I'm getting the door," I mumble to myself since no one is near enough to hear or probably care.

I came straight home after speeding away from Dmitri like a scorned woman, which, of course, I'm not. I may have overreacted—a tad. I don't have the heart to tell my siblings that we lost the Storm job. Maybe after dinner when they've had a few beers.

My brain stutters to a stop when I open the door to the man on my mind. "Mr. Storm?"

He steps forward with arms full of takeout. "You can be mad at me, but please call me Dmitri or Dima." He lifts the bags. "I think these are yours, according to the guy I met on the way up."

"Here. I'll take those." Gavin steps before me and grabs the food from Dmitri, giving him a half-hearted smile before sending me a questioning look and slipping away just as quickly.

Silence envelops us as we stare at each other, Dmitri in his dark slacks and white button-down. He lost his jacket and rolled up his sleeves, showing off his muscled forearms—again—that have me thinking dirty—*again*. And me in my cutoff shorts and slouchy t-shirt. We're a mismatched pair to be sure. But by the heat in his eyes as he scans my legs up to my face, I don't think he much cares.

"What are you doing here?" I find my voice, and though I might regret stomping off like a petulant child, he's still insinuated himself into my life way more than a client—ex-client—should.

"Give me ten minutes—"

"Have you eaten?" My mom didn't raise me to be a dick. I cultivated that gem all on my own. He brought the food up, after all.

"No, I had hoped to take you out earlier…"

I motion him inside. "You'll have to forgive me. My brother will hound you and my sister… Well, I have no idea what she'll do or say."

We make it five feet into the kitchen when my sister turns, a wicked smile spreading across her face as she sashays toward Dmitri. "Well, who are you, handsome? Are you my dessert?"

Chapter
NINE

WITH CAT-LIKE REFLEXES, I CAPTURE THE sister's wrist before she can touch me. "Don't. And no," I sneer.

Her fingers twitch in my grasp, seconds from trailing up my arm as she devours me with her eyes.

Releasing her, I step to Casandra's side, gripping her hip, pulling her into me, staking her claim over me. If anyone's having me for dessert, it's *mój skarb*.

"Oh well, my loss." Her sister winks and practically skips from the room.

Beside me, Cas lets out a breath, drawing my attention. "Sorry—"

I tip her chin. "You don't need to apologize. Besides, you pre-apologized." I hold up the bottle I brought as a peace offering. "Can I pour you a glass?"

Her face lights up. "You brought the good stuff."

"Only the best for *mój skarbie*."

"You're going to tell me what that means someday, right?" She grabs two glasses.

"Someday," I agree, though it seems safer for her and me if

she doesn't know. I trail her to the dining room, where her siblings are already dishing out food.

"Dmitri Storm, meet my brother, Gavin, and my sister, Scarlet."

"Mr. Storm, it's an honor." Gavin stands, shaking my hand like the fine upstanding person he probably is.

"Please, it's Dmitri."

"Dmitri." Scarlet lifts her hand like a limp snake, without standing, as if she expects me to bow and kiss it.

That's a hard pass. I simply nod my hello and pull Casandra's chair out for her to sit. I find overtly flirtatious women are best ignored; any attention is likely to encourage Scarlet. Plus, it's rude of her to hit on me when I'm obviously here for her sister.

When Zeke gave me her address, he mentioned her siblings lived with her. Now that I see the huge four-bedroom flat, I'm wondering why. It's obvious Casandra is doing well for herself. The deed is in her name. In fact, the whole damn building is in her name. She doesn't need roommates to help with rent.

Perhaps they need her.

I resist the urge to kiss Casandra's shoulder as she sits. I do, however, trail my finger along the spot my kiss would have landed. Her intake of air has me smiling, but I quickly reel it in. I'm supposed to be apologizing, not gloating over our mutual attraction. That'll just anger her all over again, and for the moment, for whatever reason, she's given me a reprieve. I'll not squander it on minor wins when it's the war I'm determined to take.

"Your home is beautiful," I offer as I sit beside her, eyeing the takeout containers from a Greek restaurant around the corner.

"Thanks." She hands me a container of beef or maybe lamb. "Dig in. We've bought enough for a small army."

"How long have you lived here?" I start to assemble a gyro with a side of rice and a chicken kabab. It looks and smells amazing.

"Five years," her brother fills in around his huge bite of gyro. "You want a beer, Mr. Storm?"

"Please, call me Dmitri. And, no, I'll stick to the scotch."

"You want water too?" Casandra asks.

"Sure—"

She slides her untouched glass of water to me before getting up.

"I can get it." I start to stand, but she waves me off.

"Sit," she insists. "Anyone need anything?"

"More napkins, please." Gavin cleans up a glob of tzatziki that missed his plate and hit the table.

I lay another napkin across my lap as I attempt my first bite, having stuffed more than is probably containable in the pita.

Damn, I groan my approval.

"Good, huh?" Gavin agrees.

"It's our favorite Greek place," Casandra chimes in as she sets down her water and extra napkins. "We probably get it once a week. We're not big on cooking."

"You should try my sister's. She makes a really good gyro too. I could drink her tzatziki."

"Ah, man, I love that stuff. I could eat it on everything." Her smile stops my heart for a second before it gallops at full steam.

"Did your sister make the bread Cas brought home yesterday?" Scarlet inquires.

"Yes, it was my grandfather's recipe," I offer more details than needed, but it feels wrong not to give credit where it's due.

"Dang. I could live off that bread and not give a shit about the extra weight on my hips." Scarlet forks a bite of salad, vigorously shoving it in her mouth.

All three of them eat like they haven't had a meal in days. I frown at the thought. Casandra said they don't cook. Maybe they haven't. But surely...

"You have to forgive us. Our dad loved food. There's not

much good he gave us, except a hearty appetite and a head for numbers." Casandra seems almost embarrassed by that fact.

"Are you geniuses like your sister?" I eye Gavin and Scarlet, watching their reactions. It might be rude to ask, but I'm curious all the same.

Casandra's eyes flash to mine, trying to figure out how I knew that. Do I tell her I had her checked out? All potential employees—contractors or not—undergo a background check. Hers might have gone a little deeper than most after our first encounter.

"We can't all be Mensa members," Gavin teases.

"You hold your own. Both of you," Casandra encourages her siblings. Has she always been more like a mother to them? Is that why they live with her?

"Dad only wished he could've played poker like—"

"Let's not air all our dirty laundry. Shall we?" Casandra cuts off her brother before he can finish his thought I'd really like to hear.

"You play poker?" I ask to avoid hard family talk.

"Poker. Twenty-one—"

"Not anymore," she talks over Scarlet, giving her a warning look.

There's a story there, I'm sure. "If you'd like to play—"

"No. Thanks," she's quick to turn me down.

If I doubted Casandra didn't like talking about herself before, I'm certain now. She couldn't look more uncomfortable if she tried.

The idea of watching her play cards at my casino, trying to beat the house or other players is enticing and settles in deep.

I drop it. For now.

The rest of dinner is filled with small talk with little substance, but Casandra's mood lifts, giving me hope I haven't ruined my chance with her, professionally or personally.

Sitting in the living room while they clean up, I sip another scotch and flip through the file she handed me after dinner. The one she was going to have sent over tomorrow. She says I need a forensic accountant, but I don't see how they could be any more thorough. My heart sinks when I get to the summary.

The ID she highlights. The name it belongs to.

"I can't prove it was actually him." She sits beside me on the couch, a refreshed drink in her hand.

"What do you mean?" His name is here in black and white.

"It only proves it's his ID. I can't prove it was actually him. Do you have cameras in the office? Can you prove he was even in those locations around the time of the transactions?"

"We have some cameras in the common areas, but I'd think he'd choose locations that weren't in the path of the cameras."

"Does he know you have cameras? Is he smart enough to think he can get away with it?"

"He didn't get away with it." I scrub my face and drain my drink.

She frowns and refills my glass. "He has so far."

"He would have if you hadn't brought this to my attention."

She shrugs. "I'm sure someone would have found the anomalies."

I'm not so sure. I'll check on the camera angle with Zeke.

"And if he's not on camera?" I prompt.

"Then it's hard to prove unless you can follow the money trail to accounts owned by him. Besides the investigation being legal and above board, that's where a licensed forensic accountant comes into play."

I eye the name again. "He can be a true asshole. He's hardly serious about work. But he wants for nothing… except maybe my reputation, my clout. I just can't see him doing this."

"Then give him the benefit of the doubt. Maybe someone working under him has access to his login. Stealing someone's

ID is easy enough. What you need to do to stop it from happening again is implement two-factor authentication. The owner of the ID will get a text message verifying the login attempt. Breaches could be identified immediately. I wouldn't do it until you're ready to take action, as you could lose the only leverage you have—if he's not the one syphoning money."

"My system is that antiquated?"

Her smile is endearing if not placating. "Yes. What this person has done is smoke and mirrors to draw you off their scent. I'm just a better bloodhound than they are a criminal mastermind."

"It sounds like you're a criminal mastermind."

She shrugs again. "I like to solve puzzles," she offers as if her finding a three-and-a-half million-dollar embezzlement scheme is no big deal.

"But you *could* be a mastermind?" Why do I find that so hot?

"Maybe. But I'm not. I've never cheated or stolen money in my life." Her insistence seems telling.

"Come work for me. I need you, Casandra Vaughn. Don't make me beg. I'll try to not be a dick." I give her my best puppy dog eyes.

She only laughs. "So, begging is a possibility?"

"You agree to take me back on as a client and that date on Friday, I'll beg. Tell me when and where."

"Hmm." She taps her lips with her finger. "Pour me another drink, and I'll think about it."

WARMTH SURROUNDS ME. DREAMS OF strong arms, a muscled chest and tender kisses knock in my memory, stronger than the actual throbbing in my brain. Slowly, I open my eyes and blink them closed a few times before I can keep them open, taking in my living room from my horizontal view. The TV is off. The curtains closed, no light seeping in.

It takes a second to realize I'm on the couch, and, by the breath on my neck and the hand on my breast, I'm not alone. I dare a glance at the thumb sweeping back and forth across my nipple. I gasp and accidently push back into the man lying behind me.

He groans and pushes his impressive length against my ass. "Don't tease," he grumbles into my neck.

Jesus. Could I make our working relationship any more difficult or embarrassing?

By the drumming in my head and the brain fog, I'm going to guess I had one or three too many scotches last night.

It's early. I think. I have to get up. Gavin or Scarlet could come traipsing into the kitchen at any moment, looking for their morning caffeine fix, and seeing our newest client with his hand on my breast is probably not the best message to send them—or the owner of such a naughty hand.

"I need coffee and the red or blue pill—whichever one will kill this headache," I murmur into the early morning light just beginning to peek through the curtains.

"Orgasms are better for headaches." His hand squeezes as his head lifts. I catch his eyes widening at the placement of his hand. "I thought I was dreaming." He slowly slides his hand to the curve of my waist. "Sorry." His head hits the cushion. "I'll make coffee while you find Morpheus' pills. Seems I've caught your headache."

With the rasp in his voice and the way his body is hugging mine, the last thing I want to do is separate from him and get up.

I have to.

Do I? Do I really? He mentioned orgasms…

"I think I need to play hooky from work," I groan, extricating myself from his deliciously comforting, dirty thought-inducing form. "I'm the boss. I can do that, right?" I make it to a sitting position, holding my head, ensuring it doesn't explode.

"Don't make me laugh." He rises, sitting beside me, his thigh resting against mine. His arm lazily lies along my back, his hand curled around my hip. "I could go for a little hooky." He one-eye smirks at me as he squints against the rising sun.

"I'm seriously not sure I can get up." I'd laugh if I wasn't sure I'd puke instead. Have I ever felt this bad after a night of drinking?

"Here, let me…" He attempts to stand, sways and falls back on the couch, taking me with him. "Let's rest right here. Just a few minutes. Then I'm making coffee. Promise."

I curl into his side. He twists, pulling me closer and the blanket we were using over us. "Ten minutes."

"Thirty, but who's counting?"

"We're the bosses. We make the rules."

"Exactly."

"I wouldn't wake them," a woman's voice penetrates my consciousness.

"He may have an important meeting this morning—" some guy replies.

"I don't think he'll care. They look cute," she sighs.

"They look like they reenacted a *Walking Dead* marathon."

"Shh," the woman in my arms shushes them. Casandra. That's who's in my arms.

"Thank you." I squeeze her tighter.

"You're welcome." She snuggles in closer. "Time?"

"Just after eight. Here." Gavin offers us cups of coffee. "I thought you could use this. Tylenol is on the table with water. There are cinnamon and blueberry muffins too."

Casandra sits, using me to push herself up, and smiles sheepishly. Her hair is sticking every which way, her makeup-free face is flushed from sleep, and she yawns as she takes a cup from Gavin and hands it to me.

"Thanks," I say to whoever cares.

Gavin hands her the other mug and takes a seat across from us. "So... you slept on the couch?"

Given we're fully dressed minus my shoes and socks, it's apparent we only slept. Not that I don't remember kisses before we passed out, or me pulling her close to rest on my chest as I laid us down on the couch. I should have left after two drinks. But I was in her space, and she was in mine, and before I knew it, it was late, we were drunk, toeing the line between teenage flirtation and full-on dry-humping on the couch.

And it was... amazing.

I sit up, blow on my coffee and ignore Gavin's question. It's really none of his business.

Casandra seems to have the same idea, saying pointedly, "I'll see y'all later at the office."

He nods before getting up. They putter around the kitchen a few minutes before heading out with a quick goodbye.

"Sorry about that." She side-eyes me as she sips her coffee.

"It must make having overnight guests uncomfortable," I prod.

She shrugs. "We don't typically."

My brows shoot up at that. "None of you?"

"They prefer to go other places. I'm perfectly fine with that. I'd rather not have a revolving door of strangers in my home."

I get that. "And you?"

She opens the Tylenol, handing me two pills and a bottled water before getting her own. "Yeah, I really don't."

I swallow the pills and half the water, waiting till she swallows her pills before asking, "You don't what?"

"Do that."

"Do what?" I don't want to read too much into what she's saying—or not saying. She needs to spell it out for me.

"Have overnight guests," she answers into her coffee cup before finishing it off.

"What do you do?" The idea of her going to some guy's house sets off a streak of jealousy that's foreign and unexpected.

She stands, wobbles and catches herself on my proffered hand on her waist.

"You okay?" Maybe we really should consider playing hooky.

"Yeah." She gives me a small smile before she takes my cup and empty water bottle. "I'm getting us more coffee and a muffin. Which one do you want?"

"Thanks. I'll take either or both."

She laughs. "I have eggs if you want toast and scrambled eggs instead."

"I thought you didn't cook." Standing, I find my legs a little harder to keep under me than usual.

"I said I don't cook. Not that I can't."

I follow her to the kitchen. "I'd love some eggs. Let me do the coffee while you make them?"

"Sure."

The view of her ass in those cutoff shorts revitalizes my morning wood. I adjust and take on the task of making us coffee and doctoring it the way she likes.

New coffee in hand, I watch her work the stove and wonder aloud, "Why do your siblings live with you?"

"I started looking out for them before I was old enough to be considered responsible. Our dad wasn't… Well, he wasn't around much, and our mom died giving birth to Scarlet. I'm kinda their older sister and parents wrapped in one."

"I'm sorry about your mom. That couldn't have been easy. Sounds like they've been lucky to have you."

She dismisses my compliment with a shake of her head. "I needed them too. I needed a reason to stay out of trouble."

"And did you?"

"Stay out of trouble?"

"Yeah."

She scrapes the eggs from the edges of the pan, turns down the heat, pushes the lever on the toaster, and grabs plates. "Not always." She turns to face me. "Some of my riskier decisions landed me this home."

I try not to show my surprise. "How so?"

"I'm good with numbers," she offers like it's a fully conceived explanation.

"I knew that. What did you do with those numbers?" I'm

beginning to get an idea of just how she used her intelligence to get ahead beyond her business.

"I bet on myself." She turns off the stove and plates the eggs as the toast pops.

"And the house lost?" I prompt.

"Among others." She hands me a plate, grabs hers and some forks and heads to the table.

I follow. "You don't gamble anymore?"

"You don't like to gamble unless you know you can win, right?"

I told her that our first day together over lunch. "Right."

"*I* don't like to gamble because it's not a gamble. If I play, I win."

"Always?"

She shrugs.

"You want to test that theory at my tables?"

"You could just write me a check for a million and call it a day."

I nearly choke on my bite of eggs. "Why a million?"

"Because that's the least amount I'm willing to walk away for."

"You're that confident?"

"I could take you for more, but I have a conscience, which is why I don't play anymore."

"Is that how you bought this building? In winnings?"

Her sardonic laugh is unnerving. "I should have known you'd check up on me. I assume you already know all about my dad?"

"What? No." I frown. "I just had a background check done on you, as I do all my employees or potential business partners. I don't know anything about your parents or your gambling, honest. I'm not playing games. I really don't know, but I'd like to. When—if—you want to talk about it."

Chapter
ELEVEN

I T'S BEEN DAYS SINCE I'VE SEEN CASANDRA. We've emailed and texted primarily about work and the details of meeting up tonight for our date. I've never had to work this hard for a date in my life. Considering I don't date, that's perhaps not saying much—or it's saying a whole lot.

In perfect Casandra form, she insists on meeting me at the restaurant. It's probably for the best, considering my proposal and the new line I intend on instilling between us if she agrees.

I'm nervous. I don't do nervous. It's putting me on edge, making me doubt if this is the right move with her. Once it's out there, there's no taking it back. There's no undo.

Man the fuck up. This is the only option.

I don't date.

I don't do hearts and flowers.

I don't do love.

I step onto the curb, glancing back as Sergio drives off. If all goes well, I won't need him again tonight. Casandra can take me home when she joins me for a night I won't soon forget. I do a double take when I spot her at the entrance looking uncomfortable as she smiles at guests as they enter. She backs away from the door, giving them space. I told her I'd meet her inside at the bar.

She never does as I say.

I clench my jaw and button my suit jacket. The thrill of seeing her zips along my bloodstream as I eat up the vision of her in a black halter dress, showing off her delectable shoulders and curves. She's hot as fuck. But I wouldn't mind peeling her out of those cutoff shorts she wore the other night.

Her eyes find me through the crowd. The heat of our connection steals my breath, and her smile squashes my agitation. She's stunning, captivating, a twist of intelligence and sultry stubbornness. Everything I never wanted. Until now.

"Mój Skarbie." I grip her waist, pulling her to me as I open the door. I settle for a kiss to her temple as we step inside, when all I really want to do is take an hour or two tasting her lips and exploring that mouth of hers that defies and tempts in equal measure.

"Hi." She leans in, and I cherish the trust she's giving me. She's going to need it.

"Hey yourself." I steal a quick kiss, just a moment to breathe her in and let her warmth wash over me. *She has to say yes.*

The hostess recognizes me and leads us through the throng of people to my reserved corner booth in the back. It's a perk of the job.

"I didn't want to sit at the bar by myself," she offers as explanation for waiting outside.

I'm struck by her honesty. "No one would have bothered you."

She chuckles, tapping her nails on the table. "You don't know that. You try being a single woman in Vegas sitting at a bar—alone."

Taking her in, I really consider what she just said. She's confident, beautiful, and yet there's an air of vulnerability more prominent tonight. She's right. I have no idea. "Touché."

I order a scotch and frown when she sticks to water. "I think

I had enough the other night. It might be a while before I drink again."

"Make mine a sweet tea with lemon," I change my order. If she can do tonight sober, so can I. Though, I'd rather she be a little more relaxed. A single drink would allow that for both of us.

As we wait for our drinks, I peruse the menu, though I already know what I'm going to order and what I'll recommend she try as well.

"How long do I have to wait for you to get to this proposal of yours?" She eyes me over her menu, letting it fall to the table.

Now I really wish I had that scotch. "I was thinking after dinner."

"Afraid?"

"Nervous. I really want you to say *yes*." My heart rate picks up, knowing what's on the line. The depth in which she affects me, is unnerving.

Her eyes widen and then soften with her smile. She reaches for my hand, giving it a squeeze. "It can't be that bad an offer, can it?"

"I hope not." I can't believe how nervous I am. I'm a catch. I don't *want* to be caught, yet I want to catch *her*, for as long as she'll let me.

I've got this.

Her brows rise, waiting as the server delivers our drinks. The silence is deafening. The pounding in my ears makes me wish we were someplace private—like my place.

"I don't do relationships," I start and frown when she pulls her hand away. That's not a good start.

"I suppose I don't either, not really."

"I don't date."

The shock in her brow conveys how much I suck at this.

"Is this not a date?" She frowns. "Did I misunderstand?"

"No... Well, yes. I don't want to date you. I want to fuck you." There. I've said it.

"Wow." She flinches as if I'd struck her. "That's..."

"Exclusively."

She bites her lip and looks away. "Is that supposed to make it better?"

"Yes. I'd only be with you. I'd ask the same in return."

She squints. "Is this like a *Fifty Shades of Grey* thing? With a contract and an NDA?"

"If that's what you'd like." I hadn't planned on making it official like I do my other *arrangements*, but I can see how it would be beneficial to have it all out in the open, clean, laid out. No misunderstandings.

"Are you a Dom? Are you expecting me to submit to you?" Her distaste for this proposition is growing by the second.

"No." I clasp her hand. Thankfully, she doesn't pull away. "I'm attracted to you. I think we would be great together. You can't deny we have chemistry."

"Chemistry." She nods and looks around the room.

She told me previously what she thought of chemistry: not all chemistry is good. But she and I are—

"Do you think anyone else in here is having this bizarre conversation?" She motions to an older gentleman and a young woman. "Do you think he only wants her for sex?"

"That's not—"

"No?" Her gaze slides back to mine. "I thought you liked me."

The hurt in her eyes has my heart lurching. She's misunderstanding and going to say *no*.

"—we had a rough start, but after the other night, I thought..." She shakes her head, holding her hand up, closing her eyes for a split second before she stands. "Excuse me." She grabs her handbag and walks away.

Why is she always walking away from me?

He only wants me for sex.

How stupid am I for thinking we could possibly be more?

I had to leave before I made a scene. I don't want that kind of attention, especially not with such a well-known man as Dmitri Storm. My professional reputation would be worse than Scarlet's.

The man needs a warning label: *Likely to cause completely sane, rational women to become emotional wrecks, quick to anger, and highly susceptible to murderous thoughts.*

I'm embarrassed at how badly I misread the entire situation. He doesn't want me for me, but me for my body. Which, if I'm being completely honest, isn't all that great. I mean, it's fine. I like my body. But I'm not a Victoria Secret model men only see as a sexual object. In my line of work, men don't see me in that light—at all.

Should I be flattered?

I'm not. I'm incensed. Livid. And utterly hurt.

Humiliated.

My lip trembles and I bite back the tears.

How could I be so wrong about feeling a connection, something more?

"Hey. Hey, Casandra, wait." Mr. Tall, Dark, and Bossy grips my arm a second before I turn the corner and escape him entirely.

"Don't." I twist out of his hold, picking up my pace. "I have nothing to say to you." I have to get away before my tears begin to fall.

"I have plenty to say to you—"

I spin, causing him to crash into me, but I'm ready. I push

him back. "Really? I think you've said enough." I push him again, advancing. "Let me be perfectly clear. I don't want just a sexual relationship with you. If that's all you're offering." I point into the night. "Go find yourself a hooker. She's in the right headspace to accept your offer, and the money you'll pay will buy her silence to put up with your ginormous ego."

I walk away, not caring if he follows or reaches out to me. I have no intention of speaking to this man again. *Ever.*

Chapter
TWELVE

THE NEXT DAY

Me: *Give me a chance to explain.*

Mój Skarb: *Not interested.*

THE NEXT NEXT DAY

Me: *I sent you a delivery.*

Mój Skarb: *I threw it in the trash.*

Mój Skarb: *Don't waste your time, money, effort.*

Mój Skarb: *I don't want to speak to you.*

Mój Skarb: *Lose. My. Number.*

Mój Skarb: *Forget I exist.*

THE DAY AFTER THAT

Me: *There's a delivery for you. It can't be returned. It's too big to throw away.*

Mój Skarb: *I can't be bought.*

A picture comes through a few hours later of a woman in the car I bought for Casandra.

Mój Skarb: *Cecelia, our intern, says thanks for the car.*

Mój Skarb: *Lose. My. Number.*

Mój Skarb: *Forget I exist.*

As if I could.

ONE WEEK LATER

Me: *I'm not giving up. Plus, you have a system to support.*

Mój Skarb: *I'll send Gavin to uninstall it.*

Me: *Don't you dare!*

Mój Skarb: *Fine. I'll send Scarlet.*

TEN DAYS LATER

She actually sent Scarlet. I walk into my office to find her perched on my desk like she owns the place—or more like she's fucking the guy who owns the place, filing her nails, looking all kinds of bored.

"What are you doing here?" I bark and slam the door.

"I hear you're looking for a sex slave."

"What?!" I halt in my steps. Did Casandra really tell her that?

She sighs. "Seriously?" She gets to her feet. "I hear you have a glitch that needs looking at. That big guy told me to wait in here."

"Zeke?" Why would he tell her that?

"I don't know. He's yea high," she reaches over her head, "and built like a brick house. Kinda hot in an inbred kinda way."

Kurwa! Fuck! She has some balls on her. Reminds me of her sister. "How's Casandra?"

Her brows rise as if my question is out of line. "She's sad. I don't know what you did, but you royally fucked up for her to send me in her place."

I scrub my face. "Yeah, don't I know it."

"What'd you do?"

"It's not my place to say." Actually, it is, but if feels like a betrayal to share the details with my treasure's sister.

"You fuck around on her?" She leans over my desk, getting in my face. "I typically don't care who a guy screws, unless it's my sister." She stands up and saunters to the door. "You should be more careful who you *screw* over."

She opens the door to leave.

I jump up. "Wait. Aren't you going to look at our system?"

She shrugs. "I fixed it thirty minutes ago. I just stuck around to fuck with you."

And just like that, she's gone.

A moment later I get a text.

Unknown number: *I wouldn't hit the space bar on your laptop if I were you.*

Fuck. Fuck. Fuck.

TWO WEEKS LATER

"You're grumpy as hell." Zeke hands me a scotch, which I quickly set aside.

Casandra has ruined my favorite drink for me. How is that even possible? It's been weeks of silence. I've seen Scarlet. Even Gavin stopped by for a pity check-in.

But no sign of my Skarb.

She doesn't even answer my texts any longer.

Did she block me?

When I stop by her flat, no one answers.

When I stop by her office, she's amazingly out every time. I even searched the last time with Scarlet looking over my shoulder, asking, "Did you get your laptop fixed?"

Crazy wench. She didn't do a damn thing to my laptop. I let it sit there for two days untouched for fear of what would happen. After two days of my tech guys staring at it with no idea how to work on it without hitting the space bar, I said fuck it and hit it.

Nothing happened.

Though, to be honest, she very easily could have done anything to it.

Thirty seconds later, I got a text from the same anonymous number:

Sucker.

She's one scary woman.

"You want me to make an appointment for you?" Zeke meets my gaze over his phone from the other side of my desk.

I only scowl. *No, I don't want a fucking appointment with the agency.* I only want one girl, and it's totally fucking with my head.

I have a good plan in place.

I still want Casandra in my bed. Only, apparently, that's not what she wants.

She wants *more.*

Actually, I'm not a hundred percent what she wants because she won't talk to me. But from the fact that she said she's not interested in *just a sexual relationship*, I'm gathering she wants it all.

I've never done *all.* I've only done parts, mainly the sexual parts. My parents had a great marriage, but that didn't turn out the best for them. My brother… yeah, he's not any better than me. And Mina, well, she's holding out for Mr. Right, but she tends to find Mr. Right Now more often than not. I don't know how she keeps putting herself out there.

It's exhausting trying to figure out how to get Casandra to even be in the same room with me, much less let me explain, apologize. I can't imagine the work it'll require to make a full-blown dating relationship work—succeed.

"It's been weeks. You need—"

"Don't." I don't need him telling me what my cock needs. I damn well know who it needs, and her name is Casandra Vaughn. "Anything else?"

"Daniel Sanchez is ready to meet—"

"Who?"

"The forensic accountant. He wants to discuss his findings."

"Set it up."

"I'll work with Max to get it on your schedule." He pauses

at the door. "The car will be here at eight to take you and your *date* to the gala."

I totally forgot. I'd hoped Mój Skarb would be the one to go with me. Instead, I've had to make other arrangements. "I'll be ready."

If it wasn't for this being my mother's charity—the one she founded years before she died—I wouldn't be here tonight. As it is, Gavin is my date. Though, technically, we're solo since we're both attending to represent our family. Scarlet is understandably absent. The evening will no doubt include some sort of tribute to Catrina Vaughn. And though no one blames Scarlet, it's still hard to be in a room where everyone knows the events around Mom's death involve you being born. It's a reminder Scarlet doesn't need. Therefore, she doesn't attend, with our blessing.

"Are you drinking tonight?" Gavin's grip on my waist tightens as he stops to grab a glass of champagne from a passing waiter.

"I'll sip." I take the offered flute as Gavin snags one for himself.

"Let me know if you prefer something stronger." The waiter smiles broadly as if he can sense I'm going to need it to make it through the night.

I've barely left the loft since my hopeful heart was trampled by Dmitri. I've worked remotely most days, only going into the office when absolutely necessary. Thankfully, I've missed his numerous attempts to see me in person. Though I do ignore his knocks when he comes to the loft.

I've since implemented a doorman and security detail,

which should have been there all along. They no longer let Dmitri up or allow him to loiter in the lobby.

He's a busy man. Surely my turning him down is not *this* important to him. You'd think I rejected his love, much like he essentially told me I wasn't worthy of his. I was only worthy of his body, his pleasure, nothing more, but I had the self-respect to want more for myself than scraps.

I wish it felt better.

"Hey. You're going to have to fake it better than that. Mr. Storm and his date just walked in." Gavin motions to the center doors where Dmitri stands, scanning the room, leaning in to talk to the striking beauty on his arm.

My heart plummets as I slink out of view. I knew I should have skipped this year. Gavin offered to handle the opening welcome speech reserved for Mom's family to deliver each year since we've been old enough to take on that task. It's really the only involvement we have with the charity besides our personal donations and attending these charity events. The day-to-day operation is left up to the non-profit CEO and board members.

"Do you want to leave?" Gavin turns to block me completely.

I smile at my brother. He'd totally leave and cause a scene for me. "No, but I might let you give the opening remarks. If you're okay with that? I can stand by your side, but I'm not sure I can keep it together to do Mom justice if I have to speak."

We were too young to attend these events when she was still with us. But I've seen videos of her opening remarks and speeches throughout the years. She was vibrant and charismatic. I'm nothing like her. Of the three of us, Scarlet would fill her shoes best. Someday, if she decides she wants to tackle it, we'll be here to support her, but for now, we do our part to keep Mom's legacy alive.

"I can do it. And, yes, I want you next to me. It's our legacy. We'll represent it together like we have every year since we turned eighteen."

He and I aren't even a year apart. My first year attending the gala was his first year too as it fell after both our birthdays.

He motions behind me. "We can head back to the green-room if you want. Relax a bit before it's time to go on."

We typically open the evening before dinner is served and entertainment begins, which should be anytime now. "Sounds good."

Chapter
THIRTEEN

I'M NAMED AFTER MY RUSSIAN GRANDFATHER on my father's side. When my father was just a baby, his family left Russia to plant roots in Poland. My mother is Polish. She grew up in the same neighborhood as my father, a few years older. The name Dmitri is not widely used in Poland, for its obvious Russian heritage, but my parents believed it was a sign of respect to name me after the man who started the bakery business in our family.

The recipes I know, the ones my sister uses in her restaurant, are his recipes, often improved by my father. It's a rich legacy I'm proud to carry, despite the political upheaval between the two countries.

Our parents moved to the States before I was born. I was baking and making deliveries when my mom was pregnant with Mina. As the baby of the family, she's always held a special place in my heart—perhaps because she's the only girl. The rivalry I have with Stefan doesn't exist with Mina, which is why she's my date tonight.

She doesn't get out of the kitchen often. She's as dedicated to her craft as my father was. As the house band plays, I twirl and glide Mina around the dance floor. My mom loved to dance, insisting her children learn the waltz, Viennese waltz, foxtrot, quickstep, and tango. I enjoy evenings like this where I can put those skills to use, imagining my mother smiling down on us from heaven, perhaps dancing right along with us with Father.

"You're almost smiling," Mina teases.

I flatten my lips to ensure that doesn't happen. Beyond the lightness in my step as we ease along the floor, my mood has been anything but light these past weeks.

"Maybe this will cheer you up." She motions behind me. "There's a beautiful woman who can't take her eyes off you."

She wants me to ask *where*, but I don't care. I'm not interested.

"Oh, she's heading to the mic."

The music stops, and everyone around us turns toward the stage. We do the same. When I lock eyes on Gavin and Casandra nearing the podium, my heart stills, along with my breath.

Gavin smiles at his sister, securing her at his side before speaking. "Good evening, everyone. I'm Gavin Vaughn, and this is my sister Casandra Vaughn. We'd like to welcome you on behalf of our mother, Catrina Vaughn, to the twenty-seventh annual Trina's Hope Charity Gala."

Applause fills the room.

Behind them, a screen drops from the ceiling, and a slideshow starts to play of a woman who can only be Casandra's mom. The resemblance is remarkable. Based on the narration, it's the origin story of how the charity was founded by Catrina Vaughn.

Mina's mouth is agape as her gaze ping-pongs between the stage and me. "Is that *your* Casandra Vaughn?"

"Yes, that's Mój Skarb," I confirm, feeling proud when I have no right.

"Oh my god! You call her *my treasure*?" She side-hugs me. "That's the sweetest—"

I half listen to her rant and the slideshow audio, staring into the face of the woman who has utterly captured me as she scowls between Mina and me. With hurt shining in her eyes, she turns to her brother, who quietly escorts her off the stage as everyone's attention remains on the screen.

I tell Mina I'll be right back and work my way through the throng of people till I get to the side of the stage. Only, it's Gavin who greets me and not Casandra. "Where is she?"

He blocks my path. "She doesn't want to see you."

"I need to talk to her, explain—"

"There's nothing she wants to hear." He motions with his chin behind me. "You're being rude to your date."

I turn to find Mina slipping through the crowd, her eyes locking on Gavin, asking, "Who's this?"

I narrow my eyes on her. Was she not listening? "Gavin, this is my sister, Mina." I step aside. "Mina, this is Casandra's brother, Gavin."

"Oh, right." She points toward the podium. "You introduced yourselves."

"Is she coming back?" I interrupt her fawning over Gavin to get to what really matters—my shit show of a fuckup.

He shakes his head. "No, man. She's not ready to see you."

Will she ever be?

I'm lost in thought as Gavin ushers us to the bar. I contemplate going after Casandra. I have no way of knowing if she's heading home. Plus, they've upped their security and won't even let me in the building without her okay.

She's doing a good job of kicking me out of her life. Though I barely had a foot in the door to begin with, it feels like I've lost way more than I thought I could for a woman I claimed to only want for sex.

Exclusive sex, which seemed like a commitment on my end. Obviously, not enough for her.

Casandra isn't only intelligent, she's emotionally

mature—far more than me. She saw right through me. I did enjoy her company, the feistiness of our encounters, the back and forth. It was more than just the sexual tension. I didn't recognize it until she took it all away: the business interaction, the texting, the phone calls, the meals with easy conversations, on top of the maddening sexual heat.

I thought I only wanted sex.

Turns out I wanted her.

In the middle of dinner, I get a text from Zeke.

Zeke: *Casandra Vaughn is on the floor.*

Attached is a photo of her sitting at one of my high stakes blackjack tables.

"I have to go," I say to Mina. She barely pulls her focus off Gavin, who's been chatting her up through dinner.

"I'll be sure she gets home safe," he offers.

I should be a good brother and privately ensure Mina's okay with that, but by the look in her eyes and the wide smile she gives me, she's more than taken with Gavin. I thank him and head out.

Zeke meets me at the casino's entrance and begins walking beside me as we break through the crowd to reach the whale tables secluded in back.

"She's up two hundred grand," he whispers as we near the partitioned-off area.

Dang, that was fast. "What did she start with?" I slow to hear him out before getting within earshot of my girl.

"Ten grand. Cash."

Impressive. Not that she could bank that much but that she had that much cash on hand.

"Has she been drinking?"

"She's on her third scotch."

As thrilled as I am to see her at my table, I'm sad to see her drinking and doing something she said she didn't do anymore—gamble. I couldn't give a shit about the money, though I am happy she's winning. I'm concerned she headed here after seeing me.

Is she trying to punish me by taking my money?

Strangely, I don't mind the idea of her robbing me blind. The fact that she's here at all tells me she cares—I've gotten under her skin just as she's gotten under mine.

Maybe I still have a chance.

There's only one other player at her table. He looks like he's doing pretty well. Though the seventy grand of chips beside him are relative, depending on where he started.

As I near, she splits her pair of aces, betting $25k each. She doesn't even flinch.

Dealer sticks at eighteen.

Casandra draws a queen.

I smirk at her double blackjacks.

That was a quick $75,000. She's up over a quarter of a million dollars, and I'm not even a bit sad about it.

I signal the pit boss to shut down the table when the dealer finishes paying out.

"Hello, Skarbie." I resist the urge to kiss her shoulder as I stand beside her, leaning against the table, my arm on the back of her chair. "You having fun?"

Her glassy eyes lock on me, flashing with intelligence and too much hurt for me to ignore and not feel guilty as fuck over. "You're shutting me down?"

"You missed dinner. Let me feed you. Then, if you still want to play, I won't stop you."

"You should go back to your date." She motions to the

pit boss. "I'd like this divided among the dealers and waitstaff working tonight." She slips off her stool, walking away without a backwards glance.

The shock on the dealer and pit boss's faces is priceless. "You heard the lady. Zeke, make sure it's done."

"Yes, sir."

I catch up to Casandra in a few strides. "My date tonight was my sister, Mina."

She stops cold, her hopeful gaze lifting to mine. "The chef?"

"Yes." Casandra remembering anything about my sister makes my chest burn with warmth. I step closer, barely grazing her hand. "I'd hoped to take you tonight, but then I fucked it all up, didn't I?"

She bites her bottom lip and nods, glancing at our hands as I run my thumb along her soft palm. Lifting her eyes to mine, she admits, "You hurt me." The crack in her voice ruptures something inside me.

"Give me a chance to make it right."

The next second her hand is on my shoulder as she lifts her foot, reaching toward her stiletto heel.

"Wait." I stop her. "I can't let you go barefoot in here. We keep the place clean, but still." I pull out my phone. "Give me a second."

I send a quick text, slip my phone into my pocket. Without warning, I pick her up, cradling her in my arms. I relish her squeal and feel of her in my arms in her sexy-as-fuck black dress, and stride toward my private elevator.

"My feet don't hurt that bad. I can walk."

I've no intention of letting her go now that I've caught her again. "I'll carry you wherever you want to go. But I thought we could have dinner at my place."

She lays her head on my shoulder. "I hope you didn't order any hoity-toity food."

I chuckle. This woman, always one step ahead of me. "I ordered grilled cheese sandwiches and fries."

She sighs, "Perfect."

Chapter
FOURTEEN

H E CARRIES ME UNTIL WE'RE IN HIS penthouse, then he gently sets me on the couch as if I'm precious cargo. Him kneeling before me to remove my shoes shatters the last of my control. A single tear slips free. I try to swipe it away before he notices, but more tears follow as my heart aches for this man who doesn't want me in any substantial way—in a way that I'm afraid to want.

"Skarbie," he whispers as he touches his forehead to mine and squeezes my thighs. "I'm sorry I hurt you. It was never my intent."

I run my fingers through his hair, resisting the urge to tug him closer for a kiss. I want to say *it's alright*. But really, it's not. "We barely know each other, but it felt like we were starting to. Then… When you said you only wanted sex… It hurt. Like I wasn't worth the time or effort for anything else than the bare minimum you'd give someone."

"Not true." He sits back, nostrils flaring, taking a few steady breaths before he meets my gaze. "It's about my shortcomings, not yours."

I consider his words, not fully trusting them—definitely not *wanting* to trust him.

Yet, on some level, I do, maybe just not with my heart.

If I was meant for him, he'd think I was worth the effort even if he believed he fell short of the mark—which he doesn't. Anyone would be lucky to be the center of his attention. And for a breath of a moment, I thought I was. But I can't make him want more with me, nor do I intend on trying. He either does or he doesn't. And it's clear he doesn't. But still… "You're selling yourself short. You have more to offer than just your body."

"There are those who would disagree."

I don't really care what anyone else believes about him. "Maybe you should only care what I think."

We stare into each other's eyes for a long time. Over the skirt of my dress, he rubs my thighs. His thumbs swipe back and forth. It's comforting, not sexual. Though it could easily tip the other direction. I'm not sure which way I want to fall.

When my stomach growls, the moment is broken. With a soft smile, he stands, offering me his hand. "Food will be here any minute. Let's get you something to drink."

I place my hand in his. "No alcohol, please."

He chuckles. "I don't know. You won $275K while drinking scotch. I'd say alcohol doesn't diminish your capacities in the least."

I don't tell him I probably would have doubled my winnings if I hadn't been drinking and emotional over seeing him on a date after he told me he *doesn't date*. I felt lower than low. I wanted to hit him where I thought he'd feel it most—his pocketbook. Again, not thinking clearly as his pockets run deep, and my piddly winnings wouldn't have made a dent big enough for him to feel it.

"$265K. I started with ten," I clarify.

He frowns and types out a message on his phone. "Sorry, just something I need to take care of quickly."

"No problem." I walk to the bank of windows. I didn't get to really check out his place the last time I was here, with him having his tongue down my throat and all. It's a beautiful home. My eyes catch on the pool, the water shimmering in the moonlight and the reflections of Sin City, whose lights rarely dim.

"Would you like to swim?" He pushes the patio doors open, offering his hand in invitation.

I step out with him. The outdoor space is nearly as large as the inside with the pool, deck, and outdoor kitchen. "Too bad I don't have a swimsuit."

He kicks off his shoes and pulls off his socks. "Who says we need swimsuits?" He arches a brow in challenge as he continues to remove his clothes.

"What about the food?" I shake my head, surprised I'm worried about missing food instead of protesting about skinny-dipping with this man. Priorities.

"Zeke will put it in the warming tray for us. He's discreet."

"You have naked swim parties here often, do you?"

He opens his mouth to reply, but I quickly raise my hand. "Please." Dear Lord. "Don't answer that."

He's a billionaire ten times over. He lives on the Vegas strip. He owns a casino destination resort, and lives in the penthouse. He probably has orgies for breakfast and ménage à trois for dessert. I doubt there's much he hasn't seen or done.

What's one more naked girl in his pool? I'm nothing but a body to him—just another set of tits-and-ass. You've seen one. You've seen them all.

I'm nobody special, especially not to this man. The pang in my chest hurts at the reminder. "I've changed my mind. I'll take that scotch."

His fingers stop on the last button of his shirt, his brow drawn in consideration. "You sure?"

"Yep." I pop the *p*, going for casual indifference, when in fact, the sinking in my gut makes me want to puke.

It doesn't matter what I do. I'm no one special. Just another notch on his belt full of other notches.

Maybe he should be one on my belt too—my non-existent belt from the string of lovers I've never had. I'm not a virgin, but I'm not… *him.*

He nods, leaving his shirt open and his pants undone as he strides inside.

Before I can chicken out, I lose the dress, panties, and bra, diving into the deep end before he can spot me shedding my moral fiber and good sense.

I'm nobody to him beats against my heart, hardening it, reminding it to stay out of whatever happens tonight.

It's just sex.

I'm only a body.

I'm nobody to him.

When I break the surface, he's there. His pensive face is focused on me, crouching with a bottle of Macallan sitting beside him and a glass three fingers full dangling from his hand.

It's not fair how sexy he is. Dripping wet, he'd still be ten times hotter than any man I've ever met. Actually, him dripping wet might be my downfall.

As I swim forward, his eyes remain on mine. He doesn't even sneak a peek at my nakedness highlighted by the shimmering water. He barely blinks.

I'm nobody to him. You've seen one—you've seen them all.

I grasp the edge between his feet and lift up, my toes against the wall helping. Tipping my chin, I open my mouth. Waiting.

He scans my face, looking for secrets or perhaps tracing my makeup as it runs down my cheeks. Either are possible. His free hand grazes the line of my jaw. "How are you this beautiful?"

Pang. My heart skips, and my hope blooms.

They're just words. He doesn't mean it. "Sweet talker. Now, share your drink." I tip my head back again, rising to meet the edge of his glass.

This time, his eyes dip lower as the glass meets my mouth. His tongue runs along his bottom lip as if he can taste the liquor as I take two long swallows.

"What are you doing to me, Skarbie?" he asks on a whisper as if he's not really asking at all.

Ignorance is bliss. As much as I want to ask what that word means, I don't. If it's bad—if it's good—my heart can't take it. It's teetering already. One wrong move and it'll fall.

I smile with indifference I don't feel. "I'm drinking your Macallan, swimming in your pool, waiting to eat your food. If you're lucky, I'll fuck you before the night's over." I push off, turning my back, swimming to the other side to stare into the illuminated sky like those words mean nothing to me, like I'm a one-night-stand girl, *knowing* if anybody is getting fucked— it's me.

I hear the splash seconds before the lapping water hits my back. Bubbles ripple up my backside as he surfaces behind me, so close he could have run his nose up my ass and back as he ascended. His hands land on the ledge on either side of me, pressing forward, his hard length prominent between us. Goosebumps ripple across my skin.

"Mój Skarbie." He kisses up my shoulder to my ear.

I gasp as cool water drips off him and races along my skin in complete contrast to his warmth. My nipples harden, setting off tremors as I lean in, wanting more.

He presses back, whispering, "Do you still want to know what *Mój Skarbie* means?"

"No." *Yes. But no.* I catch his gaze over my shoulder. His mouth at eye level is utterly devastating.

"Shame." He bends, brushing his lips against mine.

I turn wrapping my arms around his neck, diving in, kissing

him fully. I'm tired of holding back, pretending I don't want him—even if it's only for one night, and it's only my body he desires.

His arms engulf me, protecting my back from the side of the pool, kneading my curves, delving in places that have me moaning and him groaning into our kiss. Deeper, needier, our kiss intensifies.

I wrap my leg around his hip, allowing his hard length to press against me, teasing, cajoling, seducing, taming.

"*Mój Piękny Skarbie, chcę się z tobą pieprzyć',*" he breathes across my lips.

Whatever he's saying is sexy as fuck as it rolls off his tongue with a sensual roughness that has me panting, "Yes," despite not knowing what I'm agreeing to.

He growls his approval, teasing my entrance before hitching my leg higher and sliding a finger inside me. He feasts on my mouth, murmuring such deliciousness in his Slavic tongue. All I can do is lick and suck at him as if I can gain understanding by consuming his words a syllable at a time.

Chapter
FIFTEEN

LUST DRIPS OFF ME IN WAVES AS I DEVOUR HER mouth and ravage her body one stroke at a time. I knew once I got my hands on her again, we'd be combustible. She's on fire, and damn if I'm not happy to burn with her, despite the fact that we're in the water, soaking wet—and yet, she's wet for me in a whole other way.

Between kisses and groans of approval, I tell her everything I plan on doing to her, in detail, as I suck her tongue and piston my fingers in and out of her glorious pussy.

So sexy.

So hot.

Except, she has no idea what the fuck I'm saying because, in my lustful state, I fall into my heart's first language—the language of my family, my heritage. I learned to speak English so early. I'm not sure why I slip into Polish when my dick is hard or my temper flares.

"Mój Skarbie, let me have you," I pant against her mouth, breaking our kiss. I grip the side of her neck to capture her glassy gaze because I need her to be here with me for this.

Fuck, is she drunk? Can she even give consent?

"Are you drunk, baby? Do you know what you're doing?"

I start to pull away, considering I've taken this too far with a woman who's had more than a few drinks.

She grips my wrist, forcing my fingers I've started to pull out back inside her warm haven. So. Fucking. Sexy. "Yes, you can have me—for tonight."

I hate that she feels the need to specify an expiration for our tryst. I'm the ass who put that stipulation I don't even want between us. Tomorrow, I will set her straight. Tonight, I want her unencumbered by what crossing this line means for us.

"Yes, I know what I'm doing. I'm not *that* tipsy." She releases my wrist and pulls me closer with a grip on my shoulder. "I'm sure. Are you?"

If only she knew what my dirty mouth has been saying, she'd never ask that. Instead, she'd ask what's taking me so long to get on with it. "Never more certain, Skarbie."

"Good. Then fuck me already." She grips my ass, pressing forward, eliminating all doubt about what she wants.

Despite having reservations about taking her in the pool for our first time, her fire is hard to resist. The more she grinds on my hand and my cock between us, the harder it is to have a sane thought that isn't saturated in pheromones and packed with lust.

I pull back again, trying to slow this rollercoaster before we jump the tracks. But she's not having it. Gripping my cock, she flexes her hips to dislodge my fingers and runs the head of my cock along her seam. "Please, Dmitri, don't make me wait," she pants, the air between us thick with intoxicating want.

The feel of her on the tip of my cock. I can't even… "Never." Squeezing her ass, I surge inside her, eating up her cries of pleasure as I groan at how perfect she feels. The cool water laps at my balls as I thrust deeper, harder, the resistance making it feel like slow motion despite the speed I'm pistoning into her.

Needing more leverage, I hold her in my arms, still inside her as I walk us across the shallow end till I reach the steps. I ascend enough to rip a cushion off the nearest lounger and lay it on the deck and over the pool's edge, letting it dip into the water. Too frenzied to think beyond protecting her back, I lay her down on the cushion. Rising above her, my feet still on the steps, I sink deeper and curse her name for being so inviting and unforgettable.

I knew that. Didn't I?

It's why I wanted her. Why I made the proposal I've never made anyone that wasn't with an agency for the sole purpose of getting my rocks off.

But this. Fuck.

This is so much more than an *arrangement*.

There's no coming back from this—from her.

Gripping her hips, I thrust over and over, devouring her with my eyes as she arches, moans, and gasps under my touch, making me harder, making me forget all control, sanity, and defensive walls she managed to knock down without even trying. She's pushed me away with her false indifference. Trying to pretend being naked in my pool, drinking my best scotch, offering her body on a platter didn't mean anything to me—or her.

It means everything.

More than I'm ready to admit.

And a hell of a lot more than she's ready to hear.

"*Mój Piękny Skarbie*," I pant, leaning forward, using my weight to drive my passion into her. I'm overwhelmed by the emotion in her eyes before she blinks it away, still trying to hide from me. But she can't hide her body's response. How her sweet pussy swallows my cock, holding on when I retreat and sucking me back when I drive forward. Warm. Hot. And so fucking wet. "*Taka piękna cipka. Jeszcze piękniejsza kobieta.*"

"I don't know what you're saying, but it's hot. Don't stop." She moans, gripping the back of my neck, pulling in for a searing kiss.

Someday I'll tell her, when she's ready. But for now, between kisses, I rain my native tongue across her body, praising, worshiping, promising. She'd blush if she understood a single word.

As she grips me tighter, her legs wrapped around my hips pulling me tight, I change the angle of my thrust with a hand below her ass, raising her up. She shudders and shakes when I hit my target.

"*To wszystko, kochanie.*" *That's it, baby,* I praise as she cries out and starts to come. "*Takie piękna.*" My beautiful, beautiful girl. I seal my mouth to hers, stealing her pleasure as she squeezes me and takes me over the edge.

I come so hard, I see spots.

Breathless, I don't stop. Not until she stills in my arms and I've filled her with every ounce of my release.

Trailing kisses along my jaw, her hands run down my back to squeeze my ass, causing my hips to flex and my cock to surge. She gasps, giving me ideas for round two, before she squashes it with her body's other need. "Do you think the food is here?"

I bark out a laugh before I can stop it. "I'm sure it is." If not, someone's head will roll, but not before I find something to feed my girl.

I groan as I break our connection. Offering her my hand, I help her to her feet before stepping out of the pool and grabbing towels from the storage chest. I hand her one, wondering if she'd let me dry her off. Instead, I wrap a towel around my waist and watch as she dries her feet and legs, hiding her luscious curves behind a layer of fluffy whiteness. She wrings the water out of her hair and finger-combs it, smiling shyly when she catches me watching.

My chest pangs at the lost contact—the feel of her body against mine. I could have gone a few more times before needing to refuel.

There's time. We have all night.

Chapter
SIXTEEN

GRIPPING MY HAND, DMITRI LEADS ME INSIDE his dimly lit living room. "Sit, Mój Skarbie." He motions toward the couch, releasing my hand. As I sit, he trails his fingers over my shoulder as he passes, heading for the kitchen. Goosebumps erupt. "There's a blanket behind you if you get cold."

I twist around, running my fingers along the cording of the sofa pillow, trying not to stare at his sculpted back and bite-worthy ass as he walks. "Do you have something I could use to take my makeup off?" I'm a little scared of what I'll find when I look in the mirror. I'm barely able to meet his eyes when he turns, catching the direction of my focus.

"You're beautiful, Cas," he throws out like it's nothing. Maybe compliments come easy to him, yet he doesn't strike me as a man who gives them often.

And *Cas?* He's never called me that before. I like it way more than I should.

He motions down the hall. "First room on the right is where my sister stays sometimes. You're welcome to anything in the closet or bathroom."

I jump up—

"Though, I wouldn't mind you staying naked. I have every intention of devouring you as soon as we've eaten."

My heart flutters, and my girly parts throb at the thought of feeling him surge inside me again. I stutter my step and smile. As usual, he takes the air from my lungs, thoughts from my brain, and coordination from my limbs, yet I do manage to say, "I'm looking forward to dessert."

"Me too." He continues to the kitchen but raises a brow when I don't immediately move. "Do you need help?" His eyes flash with amusement.

"No," I squeak and shoot off to pillage his sister's sometimes-bedroom.

I lose all composure around him. A man has never affected me like he does.

It's good.

It's amazing.

It's scary as all—

I gasp when I see my raccoon eyes in the mirror. I turn on the hot water and laugh in disbelief as I search for supplies to strip my face of my war paint.

When you've seen one, you've seen them all. He didn't even notice my horrendous state.

He called you beautiful, my hopeful soul reminds me.

He lied to be polite. It's as simple as that.

I find makeup remover and cotton pads and get to work, hoping his sister has a brush in here too. It looks like a bird nested in my hair.

Seen one. Seen them all. I sigh.

My steps are heavier, my post-sex glow a little tarnished when I stop in the kitchen. Dmitri is still in his towel and looking all too relaxed and sexy when he slides a plate toward me. The reality of what this man wants from me—or doesn't want—steals the joy I felt from our… joining? I frown, not sure what to call it. I guess it was just a hookup—a notch.

"Do you want to eat at the bar, dining room, couch, outside?" he asks.

I twist my mouth, considering, unable to ignore the heaviest of options bearing down on me. "Should I go?" *You got what you wanted.* I don't want to overstay my welcome because he feels obligated to feed me.

He steps into my personal space, gripping my chin. "What happened in the minutes you left to wash your face," he scans my head, "and fix your hair? I thought we were having fun."

Fun? Yeah, I'm a blast. A regular one-night-stand joyride. "I suck at this."

His forehead creases, then he kisses me, softly, gently before pulling back. "I think you're rather fabulous at this."

"I looked like a raccoon."

"You look beautiful."

"You need your eyes checked."

"You need to learn to accept a compliment, Mój Piękny Skarbie." He kisses my cheek before releasing my chin.

I push out a puff of air. "Fair point." I do suck at taking compliments, unless you want to talk about my computer skills, then yeah, I'll eat that shit up all day. I pick up my warm plate and glass of ice water. "Lead the way."

If I'm staying, I'm definitely eating this grilled cheese. I've been fantasizing about it since the last time he fed me. It looks and smells delicious, and I'm starving.

With a quick nod, he grabs his food and drink and walks to the living room, taking a seat on the long couch I was on earlier. I would have bet this man only ate in suits in the dining room, and never grilled cheese and fries while only wearing a towel on his couch.

Situated on the couch facing him, I take a huge bite of my

crunchy goodness and groan my approval. I cover my mouth to exclaim, "So good."

"Mina makes the best grilled cheese. They're even better fresh and hot."

I can't image them tasting better than this. But my mind doesn't stay on the yummy food. My thoughts drift to outside and what took place there and *who* might have seen us. "Do you think he saw anything?" I blush at the thought of Zeke seeing us in the pool, or worse, outside the pool.

"Zeke is discreet." He doesn't even question who I'm referring to.

I cringe. "But do you *think* he saw us?"

"I don't know. Would it be so bad if he did?"

Not wanting to make a bigger deal of it, I shrug, dipping a fry in ketchup and avoiding eye contact.

"If it makes you feel any better, we were probably still in the pool when he delivered the food. With my back to him, my body would have hidden yours."

It does help—a little. But it doesn't mean I won't go out of my way to avoid Zeke the next time I see him. *If* there is a next time. Our working relationship is practically done, except for maintenance now and again, but I can do that remotely or send Gavin or Scarlet, or any of my highly trained employees. Dmitri hasn't agreed to a full system overhaul. So, I don't have to see him again if I don't want to—or if *he* doesn't want to, which means seeing Zeke again is a nonissue.

The reminder of what this is between Dmitri and me sets off an ache in my chest and a knot in my stomach. I hide behind stuffing my face and force myself to focus on other things. "Tell me about your family. Where did you grow up?"

Something resembling pain flashes in his eyes before he smiles. "I grew up in New York. My father had a bakery. My mother helped, but the baking came from his side of the family.

My grandparents moved from Russia to Poland. They had a bakery there. My parents moved to New York before I was born. I'm the oldest, then my brother, Stefan, and Mina is the baby."

"You speak Polish?"

"Yes, and Russian and French."

"And your family? Are they still in Poland and New York?"

He sets his empty plate on the coffee table, wipes his mouth and tosses the napkin on his plate. "Stefan and Mina are my family."

Oh. So that means—

"I may have cousins in Poland. My parents didn't keep in touch with family there. I'm not sure what brought them to the United States. I just know they came here for a better life."

I motion around his penthouse. "I imagine *this* is definitely a better life."

He cracks a smile for half a second. "Perhaps, but my parents were happy in their apartment above the bakery. We never needed much. We had love. We had each other."

It sounds like he had a happy childhood, but my heart hurts for what he's not saying. Are his parents dead? "It's just me and my siblings too. I told you my mom died giving birth to Scarlet. My dad… he gambled. Too much. He got himself killed owing the wrong people."

He frowns. "Did he gamble in my casino?"

I shrug and set my plate next to his. "He tended to stick to the lower-caliber casinos. Though, he probably stuck his foot in here a time or two."

"How long ago?"

"Three years."

"I'm sorry."

I sigh and get up to take our plates to the kitchen. "He got what he deserved. He was a shitty father. He'd rather hock everything we had than put food on the table and keep a roof over our heads."

"Did he teach you how to gamble?" He follows me to the kitchen.

"No. I taught myself. I was good at it. Way better than him, which only pissed him off."

"But you don't gamble anymore?"

"No." I dump my uneaten food in the trash. "Well, sometimes to let off steam." It relaxes me. The numbers, the sounds of the casino, the chance that's not really all that much of a chance if you know when to walk away. Something my father never learned. "My winnings put us through college, funded my business, bought me my building." And a few other things. It's enough. I don't need to gamble anymore. "I showed my father I was better than him. I did what he couldn't."

"Walk away?" He catches my hand and tugs me to him, taking the plate out of my hand to set on the counter.

"No. Win." I sound smug, but it's truly a fact that hurts. I didn't choose to be better at it than him. I just was. I couldn't help it. Numbers come naturally to me. But the fact my father didn't have any remorse or guilt over leaving us hungry and barely clothed with a roof over our heads, made it hard not to gloat when I did win and then did the right thing with the winnings.

"Why is your intelligence so hot?" The heat in his gaze tingles along my skin as he pulls me flush against his now tented towel.

I laugh as nerves strike, wondering what he has planned. "Is it dessert time?"

"I believe it is."

Chapter
SEVENTEEN

"C AS," HE GROANS, TIGHTENING HIS GRIP on my hair. "What are you doing to me?"

Probably nowhere close to what he's doing to me, working his way past my walls. I was determined not to let hope in, to keep him at arm's length, only a notch on my new belt. But the warmth of his eyes as he watches me suck his cock is not the way you look at a one-night stand. Though my experience is limited in that department.

Maybe he does see me.

Maybe I'm not just another set of tits and ass.

Maybe he wants more...

"*Moja Królowo, zabijasz mnie,*" he growls.

My insides contract, and I moan around him at the sensation and the memory of him speaking Polish as he thrust inside me. I release him with a pop and breathlessly ask, "What did you say?"

He lifts me off my knees and deposits me on the bed, crawling over me. "I said, *zabijasz mnie.* You're killing me." He crashes his mouth over mine, growling at what I can only assume is the taste of his precum on my tongue.

"You said more than that," I pant between kisses.

He growls again, positioning me higher on the bed,

spreading my legs with his and surging forward, filling me in one steady drive. I grip his shoulders as I rock into him, trying to steal air through his merciless kisses and riotous hips.

"*Daj mi swoje serce, bo już zdobyłaś moje,*" he demands.

"I don't know—"

"*Bądź mója.*" He lifts my leg and pushes deeper, thrusting at a pace that has my heart ready to explode along with my body. "*Bądź mója,*" he says again with more force.

I don't know what he's saying or asking, but it feels like he needs an answer. "Yes," I gasp.

"*Bądź mója.*"

"Yes."

"*Moja,*" he growls, pinching my nipple, raising my hips with a hand on my ass.

"Yes!" I cry, shattering.

"Mine," he chants as I come and come and come. "*Moja.*" Two more thrusts and he's groaning his release, breaking our kiss and mumbling, "Mój Skarbie, Moja Królowo," into my neck.

I'm loose-lipped when I'm hot for her, My Treasure, My Queen. Balls deep, I admitted she's already stolen my heart, asking her to give me hers. Of course, she has no idea. The only thing she heard was me claiming her as mine. Not understanding all the times I asked her to be mine before she said *yes*.

She has no idea what she's agreed to.

I intend on showing her.

After a quick shower to clean up and rinse off the pool water, I toss her on the bed and settle in for a midnight snack of pussy and… pussy. "*Taka piękna cipka.* Such a beautiful pussy." I kiss up her inner thigh, licking up her seam before spreading her wide. "*I to wszystko jest moje.* All mine."

"Dmitri." She squirms under my heated gaze.

Is she embarrassed? "Mój Piękny Skarbie." I kiss her thighs, encouraging her to relax. The last reprieve she'll get before I taste her coming on my tongue.

The first real taste of her pleasure has me ravenous, diving in for more—for everything. Legs over my shoulders, she pins me in place with her heels on my back as she spreads her knees wide, flexing her hips, rubbing her beautiful cunt across my face.

"*Moja.*" Mine.

I claim her with every lick, suck, plunge of my fingers, hold of my hands and body to keep her in place as I take her and take her till she's screaming my name, trembling against my lips, and coming on my tongue.

Again.

And again.

Hard and ready to spill, I flip her over, holding her down with my body, my thighs on either side of hers. I push my cock between her slick thighs until I find her entrance and slide home.

She cries out as I groan, "Fuck," against her neck. "I won't last, Mój Skarbie. You've got me too worked up." I promise to make it up to her in the morning or maybe a middle-of-the-night top-off. I work my hand under her to squeeze her breast, capturing her nipple between my fingers, working it like it's her clit.

"Gah, Dmitri," she gasps.

I slam forward fast, desperate, hard. On repeat.

Her skin glistens in the moonlight from her sweat and mine. The smell of sex, the sound of our joining, and her clawing at the bed feeds my hunger, driving me forward faster, harder.

Nearly.

Nearly. Fucking. There.

Tingles up my spine.

My balls and ass clenching.

Cock swelling.

Drilling. Drilling. Drilling.

"Need you to come, baby." I slide my other hand lower to put more friction on her clit with each piston of my hips.

Close.

Nearly...

My Queen arches and moans my name, sending jolts to my cock that it's *my* name on her lips as she contracts around me and comes, forcing me to work to surge back into her sweetness. Ramming in deep, I come harder and longer than I ever have.

I fall over her, panting, not moving, but groan as she continues to quake and spasm around me, holding me deep and tight, surrounded by proof of our passionate joining. I kiss up her neck and squeeze her breast, whispering "Mój Skarbie as a soft caress against her skin.

When she stills, I slowly slip out of her and fall to her side, pulling her limp body into my arms, wrapping around her, spooning her from behind. Her soft moans on each exhale as she catches her breath and the feel of her relaxing in my hold is something I never want to be without. "Stay," I offer before she can even think of leaving.

Silence rings in the air until she softly replies, "Okay," and lets out a heavy exhale as if I answered a question she was afraid to ask.

Never leave. The words are on the tip of my tongue as joy I never thought possible fills my heart at the idea of having a future with her. I kiss her shoulder. "Night, beautiful."

"Goodnight, Dmitri." Her voice is so soft, I barely heard her.

Once I get some sleep and my mind is working at full capacity and my cock is functioning, I'll reinforce my claim and my wish to keep her—if she'll have me.

Chapter
EIGHTEEN

A WICKED TONGUE AND PROBING FINGERS wake me. My moan surfaces before I'm fully awake, blinking into the darkened room. My knees fall wide, barely covered by the covers, my hand fisted in Dmitri's dark hair as I swivel my hips, chasing his glorious mouth as he licks and sucks at my clit and love lips.

"Right there," I sigh when his probing fingers hit the jackpot.

He growls, come-hithering my sweet spot again and again.

Liquid pools, and all I want is more. So, so much more. "Yes. There." My toes curl, and my legs shake. The sight of him devouring me like I'm his favorite treat is fuel to the fire he started.

When he runs a finger around my rosebud, I buck, my pending orgasm ratcheting up a level or two. His hunger grows, his sounds, animalistic and delicious, making me feel desired and treasured in a way I've never experienced, like there's no part of me he doesn't want to lick or touch. There are no yucky parts. He wants all of me.

I bow off the bed when he pushes through, fingers in both of my intimate places, alternating, pistoning in and out, combined with his lapping tongue and needy, sucking kisses.

"Please," I beg. "Please don't stop." Let me get there. I need to come. I might die if I don't.

And then he's gone. My orgasm falls away like a plummeting elevator.

"What?!" I cry out in shock and disappointment. "I was so close."

"Hold on, baby." He kisses my stomach and rises above me, turning me to my side. "I'll get you there again. I need to feel that orgasm around my cock." The gruff in his voice has me stilling my frustration. "It'll be even better. I promise."

I doubt that. That one felt like it was going to be pretty spectacular. And that's saying a lot considering all of my orgasms with him have been stellar, mind-blowing, life-affirming.

He wipes his mouth on the sheet and hooks my top leg over his shoulder, my other leg straight between his. He thrusts inside me and stills as he leans over, drawing my nipple into his mouth as he squeezes my other breast. *God, that feels good.* His hand on my ass slides lower, gliding through my wetness and to my back entrance, his finger pushing.

Is he?

"Ohmygod."

He did.

"Dmitri!" I cry out at the feeling of him penetrating my most intimate places at once.

He pops off my breast and rises up, thrusting his hips and sliding his finger in and out of me. "Have you done this—"

"No!"

He thrusts deeper. "Is this okay, baby?" He stills his hips and moves his finger, not deep but enough that I can feel it—everywhere.

It feels dirty, forbidden, and like… acceptance, like he can't love on me enough. He wants *everywhere.*

"Yes." I push my foot against his shoulder, raising my hips. "Please move."

He leans forward, and, using my leg as leverage, he abandons my breast to caress down my body, splaying his hand so his thumb can rub my clit as he begins to move. He grinds his hips at first before pivoting to flex forward, slowly, then harder, faster.

It feels like he's touching me everywhere: his fingers not inside me grip my ass, his other hand presses on my stomach as his thumb rubs my sensitive nub, and his cock. Oh, dear lord, his cock is working miracles inside me.

With me sideways, hips angled up, he pumps into me, taking me completely. "I think this might be my new favorite position," I pant, delirious from watching his dance. His features are taut in pleasure and concentration—his focus entirely on me.

He chuckles then groans. "*Mój Skarbie*, I look forward to testing that theory."

Yes. Yes, me too. Only I can't reply. I'm too consumed in his decadence, awash with the need to come, to feel him release inside me, filling me as if I'm not already full enough.

I squeeze my breasts, teasing my nipples, and he growls, "Twist them." Thrust. "That's it." Thrust. "Now pull." Thrust. Thrust. Thrust. "Fuck, baby. You're so damn sexy. I can't get enough."

His actions back up his statement as he drills into to me. My leg starts to shake, and I wrap my arm under my knee and pull it to my chest.

He falls forward, deeper, flush against my most intimate places. The warmth of his skin seeps into me, his entire body, pushing, pounding.

The quaking doesn't stop. So full. I'm in sensory overload. Tingling waves crash over me. I buck and can't keep hold of my leg that falls to his chest. He grunts, leaning against it, keeping me open to him. "*Tac, kochanie.* Give it to me."

I scream my release, seized in its grip, fearing the windows will rattle loose and the walls will collapse around us, tearing apart just like I am for him.

His jaw tight, he doesn't fall over the edge with me. Instead, he waits, eking out every morsel of my orgasm, and then gently slips his finger from my dark place. He turns me gently to fall over me, cupping my cheek with his other hand, rising, widening my legs with his knees, making room to settle in. And he pumps into me, staring into my eyes and saying the most delicious things across my lips that I don't understand but feel along every inch of my being, inside and out.

This man makes love like a tsunami. Devastating and all-encompassing.

He grinds and thrusts until my pleasure rises again, then he picks up the pace and kisses me into another orgasm seconds before he comes, filling me with every bit of his desire, satiating me in a way I've never known.

Falling. Falling. Falling for this man.

I'm so screwed.

Will it hurt when I land?

I start to drift off, only to awaken when he slips a warm cloth between my legs, tenderly washing before drying me off. After disposing of the towel, he comes back to bed and pulls me into his arms. I lay my head on his chest, eating up his affectionate touches and kisses as he whispers, "Mój Piękny Skarbie, sleep now."

The smell of coffee greets me when I open my eyes and stretch, sore in so many delicious places. I frown at the empty space beside me. But when I hear the shower running, I weigh my choices: fulfilling my coffee need or joining him in the shower.

Slipping on a white button-down from his closet, disappointed it doesn't smell like him, I decide coffee is the better choice, then bathroom, and possibly more sex, depending on what he has planned for the day. Being Saturday, I don't have plans to work, though I may need to, to keep my mind occupied if Dmitri isn't up to hanging out.

Familiar doubt creeps in. The one that the light of day brings by casting its all-too-bright light on uncertainty and things unsaid. I don't have regrets, though. Last night was amazing in so many ways I'm afraid to analyze and name.

I spot my purse on the entry table before I freeze at the precipice of the kitchen finding a dark-haired man in slacks and a button-down pouring a cup of coffee. Does he work for Dmitri?

He turns, preparing to take a sip before he spots me and lowers his cup with a sneer, raking me up and down. "You need to leave." Placing his cup down, he moves toward me, and I step back. Before I can make it far, he grips my arm, tugging me to the elevator with surprising strength.

"Wait!" I grab my purse as he drags me up the entry stairs.

"There's no waiting. You know the deal. You signed a contract. He doesn't let his whores stay overnight. I don't know how you managed it, but you need to leave before he realizes you're still here."

Stunned and speechless, I gape at him as he tosses me into the elevator, flicking a hundred-dollar bill in my direction and hitting the button for the lobby.

It's only after the doors close, I realize I'm barefoot and naked under Dmitri's shirt.

Chapter
NINETEEN

A SMILE TUGS AT MY LIPS AS I PULL ON JEANS and a t-shirt, relieved to smell coffee, which means Casandra didn't run off while I was in the shower. Yet when I step into the living room, the space feels empty. I dash to the kitchen and spot the cup of coffee on the counter but no trace of My Treasure.

My phone ringing has me dashing back to the bedroom to retrieve it from the nightstand. It quits ringing and starts again as I swipe it up and see Zeke's name on the screen.

"Hello."

"I just got a call from security. Ms. Vaughn was seen running through the lobby in tears—"

She ran after all. What the hell? I grab my wallet, keys, and rush to slip on socks and shoes as he continues.

"—barefoot, clothed in only a white button-down shirt, requesting her car be brought around as soon as humanly possible. Then she changed her mind and hopped in a cab."

"Barefoot? Dress shirt?" I half process what he's saying as I open the patio door to find her dress, bra, panties, and shoes lying on the pool deck right where she discarded them last night.

She left without her clothes. I might as well collect her

belongings before racing after her. I'm sure I don't have the full picture as to why she would run out of here practically naked. Indignation rises as I think what could have happened to make her leave in such a state. "Check if anyone accessed the elevator this morning." I hang up and pocket my phone.

I collect her clothing, worrying over what upset her, racking my brain on what, if anything, I could have done to set her off.

I've just put her belongings in a bag and move toward the elevator when it opens and out steps Zeke holding up a hundred-dollar bill. "This was on the elevator floor." He hands it to me as I enter, and he retraces his steps to join me.

I scowl at the bill. Did she drop it in her haste to leave? I pocket the money and prompt him to fill me in.

"Stefan accessed the elevator ten minutes before she appeared in the lobby," he grouses.

"Stefan?" I've been looking for that asshole for weeks. "Where is he?"

"In his suite. I've got two guys on his door ensuring he doesn't leave. But we need to hurry. He's not happy about it."

"Good." I hand him the bag for Casandra and push the button for the penthouse, reversing our direction. "I need to get the file Casandra gave me before I see him."

When the doors open, Zeke waits in the elevator as I head to my home office.

Opening my locked cabinet, I call Mój Skarb, holding the phone with my shoulder as I gather what I need and lock up behind me. Her phone goes to voicemail after only a few rings. "Casandra, I don't know what happened. I'm coming to see you, but I need to see a certain someone whom I believe you met this morning. Don't shut me out. Give me a chance to answer for whatever he said to you to scare you off." I end the call and hurry back to the elevator.

I have no intention of letting her go.

Not like this.

Not at all.

I've heard of the walk of shame, but I've never done it, at least not to this extent. I've had late nights, particularly when I used to gamble until the wee hours. But I always came home fully clothed.

I'm horrified by the looks of the early-morning joggers and dog walkers as I dash from the cab and scamper through the lobby to my private elevator, ignoring concerned looks from the doorman and security.

My phone pings with a voicemail seconds before it rings again. Dmitri's name flashes on the screen. I end the call, sending it to voicemail.

On his fourth call, I turn off my phone.

I hurry into my loft, thankful Gavin and Scarlet are nowhere to be seen. I fight to keep the words that man said to me as he dragged me out of Dmitri's apartment from the forefront of my brain. But they stuck. Two words in particular bring me back to the proposal Dmitri made weeks ago: *contract* and *whores*. I can't shake them loose. They're stuck rather tightly like a sticky note on superglue.

Before I can think too much on it, I dress and pack a bag rather unceremoniously. I have no idea where I'm going. I just know I can't be here when Dmitri shows up, and based on his first voicemail, he'll definitely be showing up—*after* he finds that lovely man who made me feel like a two-bit hooker. OR maybe a hundred-dollar hooker since that's what he threw at me like a tip for getting out of his hair so quickly. Like a hundred bucks is a consolation prize for never seeing Dmitri again.

He doesn't date.
He doesn't do relationships.
I'm such a fool. He told me.
He. Told. Me.
And I didn't listen.

I held out hope. Secretly pining to be his exception.

He came after me last night. I tried to keep my heart out of it, remembering I was nobody special to him. Then we had sex. We fucked. We made love. He held me all night.

He said I was *his*.

Hope sprang free.

Such a remarkable night.

Yet it ended horrendously.

I leave a note for Gavin and Scarlet and swipe Gavin's keys to his car. I leave him my claim ticket. He'll have to collect my car from the casino valet. There's no way I'm going back there.

Grabbing my bag and purse, I take the elevator to the garage. I slump against the elevator wall knowing I'm home-free. I don't have to face Dmitri, at least not today. Hopefully never. That thought sets off a new wave of tears, which I fight all the way to the underground parking garage.

By the time I hit the highway, my decision is made on where to hide out. Even if Dmitri knows about my other properties, I doubt he'll bother to look beyond my loft here in Vegas.

A day or two of ignoring his calls will turn him off—heck, maybe even hours.

A man like Dmitri is too busy to chase. He has *contractual whores*, and I am absolutely not one of those, nor do I have any intention of becoming one.

He doesn't date.
He doesn't do relationships.
I'm nothing special to him.
He told me. I didn't listen.

Chapter
TWENTY

THE DOOR IS OPENED BY ONE OF ZEKE'S GUYS as we approach. I step inside, Zeke on my tail as I spot my brother slumped on the couch with a drink in his hand, staring into nothingness. It's fucking nine in the morning, entirely too early to start drinking, never mind already being in this state. Though, to be honest, I'm tempted to join him.

"What the fuck did you do?" I stop across the living room from him, afraid if I get too close, I'll punch him for making my girl cry. "What did you say to her?"

His head pops up as if he didn't even hear us come in. "Who?"

"Casandra. The woman in my penthouse. You were there when she left half-dressed." I step forward and stop, shaking the visual of her hasty exit loose. I won't get anything from him if I strike him now. I make no promises to not hit him at some point. He deserves it for all the shit he's put me through, but especially for hurting Mój Skarb.

He scoffs. "You should be thanking me. She was walking around your place wearing your shirt like she owned the place. Like the fucking Queen of Sheba."

"Really? I doubt that." Cas is bold in many ways, but not in this. She's not secure in her place in my life. She would never in-sinuate she was more to me than she believes to be true. But the idea of her claiming me like that makes my dick twitch and eases the knot in my gut. I'll get her back as soon as I get *him* sorted.

He tosses his dark liquor back and sets the glass on the table beside him. "What's up with you? You never let your whores stay over."

I'm on him faster than he or Zeke can take their next breaths. I rip him out of the chair by his collar and press him against the nearest wall, my forearm stealing his air. "Don't ever talk about her like that."

"Boss." Zeke's big hand clasps my shoulder. "He's not worth it."

I shove at Stefan's chest and push off. "No. But *she* is."

"Fuck you," Stefan barks at Zeke.

"In your dreams, little man," Zeke taunts.

"I'll fire your ass!" Stefan continues to step on toes he has no business standing up to.

"Enough!" I point to the chair. "*Siadaj na dupę.*"

"English, asshole," he grumbles. Stefan never did keep up with the languages in our home. He only wanted to be seen as an American in every way. Denying his heritage was far too easy for him.

"Sit your ass down," Zeke translates.

I smirk. Zeke gives a shit about knowing what I'm saying. He learned Polish just to make working with me easier, especially when I'm pissed as hell and can't find any other way to express it.

Stefan scowls at Zeke but sits, eyeing his empty glass with a pout.

"Coffee, Boss?" Zeke asks on his way to the kitchen.

"Please." I take a seat in the chair farthest from my brother. I need the distance to rethink beating the hell out of him when he lips off again.

"Me too." Stefan isn't stupid, but he's pushing the bull taunting Zeke. They've always been like this. Zeke treats him like he doesn't deserve to be in my space, breathing the same air. Zeke treats Stefan in direct correlation to how Stefan treats me. Yet Zeke treats Mina like she's made of glass: gently and cautiously.

"*Możesz zrobić sobie cholerną kawę, mały człowieczku.*" Zeke's reply is flat and sounds more like a Russian mobster than a Polish baker.

I hide my chuckle behind my fist. I shouldn't enjoy the dance they do, but it's fucking funny.

"What the fuck did he say?" Stefan asks.

"You can make your own damn coffee, little man." I take entirely too much pleasure in their verbal sparring. Zeke's shoulders going up and down as he silently laughs isn't helping me keep a straight face.

Stefan pisses off a lot of people, but he should watch it around Zeke and my girl. "Zeke is mine, and Casandra is mine. You will treat them with respect, or you will find yourself without a job or a place to live." I pull out my phone when it vibrates in my pocket. "*Rozumiesz?*"

"Yeah, I understand," Stefan grumbles, translating that just fine. *Dupa.*

Coffee in hand, I stare at my brother, trying to remember where it all went wrong. We weren't always like this—he wasn't always such a pain in the ass. "Tell me what you said to Casandra so I know how to fix it."

He takes a sip of his own coffee that Zeke was kind enough to make for him, though I'm not entirely sure he wouldn't have spit in it. Of course, I don't mention it.

My phone vibrates again. I dismissed it the first time when I saw it wasn't from Mój Skarb. But now that I see it's from her brother, Gavin, worry rips through my body. "Hold on." I nod to Zeke to be sure he doesn't let my brother out of his sight and step into the bedroom, calling Gavin. As it rings, I note Stefan's bed hasn't even been slept in. *Where the fuck has he been?*

"Gavin?"

"Hey, Dmitri." The edge to his voice makes me think he's trying to remain friendly and not anger one of his biggest clients.

"Where is she?" I, on the other hand, don't give a fuck if I piss him off. I just need to get to my girl.

"I don't know—"

"What?!" Then why the fuck did he reach out to me?

"—she left a note saying she was taking off for a few days, and she took my car and left me the claim ticket to your valet for *her* car. What the hell happened last night?"

That's none of his fucking business. "We made up, but then she had a misunderstanding with my brother."

"What did he do?" His concern and worry are evident.

"I don't know. I'm at his place now to find out." I sigh and run my fingers through my hair. "You really don't know where she is?"

He's quiet for a moment. "You really didn't hurt her, didn't do something stupid?"

I chuckle. "If allowing my brother access to my place counts as stupid, then, yes, I'm guilty. But I swear to you, Gavin. I care for Casandra. I'd hoped last night was the beginning of something."

"Something real or just sex?"

I try not to flinch at his question. I don't know what Cas told her siblings, but it's obvious he knows something. "I was an idiot before. I've come to realize what I want with your sister has no limits. I want it all. I want her in whatever way she'll have me without end."

"That's good because she deserves to be loved, cared for, cherished."

"I want that too," I go on before he can consider that I'm not that for her. "I never have before, but I do now. So, please, tell me where she is. Help me fix this. Give me a chance to make her happy."

"She's going to kill me. I checked my GPS on my car. She's heading to California. She has a place on the beach in Dana Point. I'm pretty sure that's where she's going."

"Send me the address."

"You hurt her—"

"I won't. I'm not perfect. I don't know a thing about having a relationship or a girlfriend, but I want to try—with her," I promise.

"I'll text you the address. Let me know she's safe?"

"Of course. And, Gavin, thank you."

"I'd do anything for her. That includes burying you six feet under if you break her heart."

I chuckle at his attempt to intimidate. "And I thought Scarlet was the murderous one in your family."

He laughs. "I don't think you deserve to have Scarlet let loose on you. Don't prove me wrong."

"Not a chance. Hey, while I have you. You know the details of the investigation Casandra was working on for me—"

"The embezzlement and your brother?"

"Yeah. That. Can you work with Zeke and my computer guys to put the two-factor authentication in place for his ID?" I don't want to ask this of Cas when I first see her. I want to focus on us and not my business. But I can't let this slide any further now that I've got my brother in sight.

"Of course. Have Zeke call me when you're ready. I can do it remotely and explain how it works. Are you sure it's not your brother who's stealing from you, though?"

I let out a punch of air. "I'm about to find out."

Chapter
TWENTY-ONE

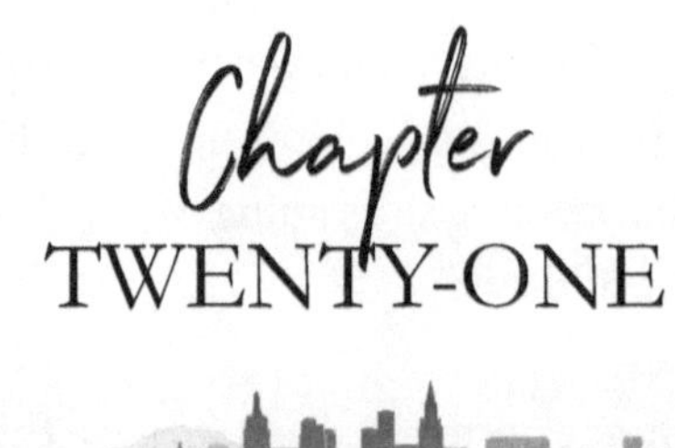

THROUGH TEARY EYES AND A STUFFY NOSE, I stare out the back porch of my beach bungalow into the surf as it crashes and lulls to the shore. I won this place off a guy in a poker tournament when I was only nineteen. Not old enough to gamble legally on the Vegas strip but legal enough to gamble in off-the-books seedy dives. Thankfully, the man I beat was a standup guy. There weren't many of those in my early days of stupid choices and questionable self-preservation instincts.

He really was pretty cool about losing this place. It was his ex's he'd won in the divorce settlement, and instead of selling it, he wanted to piss her off by giving it away. Technically, I bought it for a dollar. The yearly property taxes are insane, but it was my first house.

Gavin, Scarlet and I spent our summers here before I graduated and started my company. Now, I only visit maybe once or twice a year. I should probably sell it, but I don't have the heart to. It was the first big win that gave me confidence to keep going, except I only took cash from there on out.

I take a long pull on the Macallan I found in the liquor cabinet from the last time I was here. Was that a year ago? Sad, I can't even remember. I pay an older couple to clean the place and stock the kitchen when I know I'm coming to stay. Today, they barely had time to air the place out and grocery shop before I arrived. But the kitchen is fully stocked with all the foods I love. Though, at the moment, eating is the furthest thing from my mind.

If I keep drinking, there won't be *anything* on my mind at all. Sounds like a solid plan.

I throw back my drink and reach for the bottle, only it seems to be stuck. I tug harder on a grunt. Nothing.

"I think you've had enough." His rasp aches in my heart seconds before I turn to find Dmitri standing next to me in jeans and a white t-shirt, looking sexy as sin holding my bottle for ransom.

"Who are you to tell me I've had enough, Mr. Tall, Dark, and Bossy Pants?" I stand and step back so I can lean on a deck pillar. The world feels unsteady. Or maybe that's me.

"Mr. Tall, Dark, and Bossy Pants?" He smirks, fighting a laugh.

"Are you not tall, dark, and bossy?" I motion to him, thanking the stars I didn't call him Mr. Tall Dark and Sexy. Because that fits too.

"I suppose I am." He moves closer, the humor on his face fading as hurt flashes in his eyes. "Mój Piękny Skarbie, I'm sorry about this morning, how my brother treated you."

"What does that mean?" If this is the last time I see him, I want to know what all the things he says means. Be brave enough to ask.

He brushes his hand across my face, securing my hair. It's a lost cause with the breeze, unless he's going to stand here all day holding my hair back. "Come sit with me, and I'll tell you anything you want to know."

"Anything?"

He nods, offering his hand. "Anything, Mój Piękny Skarbie. My Beautiful Treasure."

"Is that—"

"Yes, I've been calling you *my treasure* from the moment I saw you. Different forms, but all reference you as my treasure or my queen."

From the moment he saw me? "But you thought I was somebody else."

"Who you were or weren't had no impact on how you affected me—how I *saw* you. I wanted you then. I want you now."

I slide my hand in his, watching as his fingers curl around mine. "You want me?"

"More than ever."

"But your brother—"

"Is an *idiota*."

"Idiot?"

"Yes." He tugs me toward the door. "Come talk with me, Moja Królowo. My Queen."

Treasure. Queen. "You've been sweet-talking me all this time?"

"From the moment I saw you, I was struck by all the ways I wanted to love you, despite having no idea how to do that." He holds the back door, waiting for me to pass.

"But you said you don't date. You don't do relation—"

"I'm an *idiota* too."

"It must run in the family."

He chuckles. "Apparently it does. Don't tell Mina. She'll be offended."

"Wait." I follow him to the kitchen. "That was your brother Stefan this morning? The one stealing from you?"

"Allegedly."

"Right. Allegedly." I bite my lip.

"He swears it wasn't him. He can be an asshole—*dupek*, but I believe him. He has everything he needs. He wants for nothing other than proving he's a better man than me. Financially, he has no reason to steal from me."

"Stealing isn't always about financial gain. I won money from you only to give it away."

"You were hurt and angry."

"I was—" I frown, "—am." Aren't I? The sadness I feel and the hope to see him here makes that hurt and anger seem further off than it was a few moments ago. I never expected him to come after me.

"Here." He hands me a glass of water. "You need to hydrate. Do you have any Tylenol or Advil?"

I point to the cabinet to the left of the stove. "Why are you taking care of me?"

"I take care of what's mine." So simple. So certain.

I swallow the pills he hands me and down most of the water.

"Have you eaten?" He takes my glass, refilling it.

"No. Have you?" Wait. "Are you saying I'm yours?"

He sets my glass on the counter and stands before me. "I'd like you to be. In my heart you are. I know I've fucked up. There are things to discuss, but in the end, I don't plan on leaving here without you."

"What if I say no?" Am I crazy?

"Then I'll camp on your doorstep until I win you over."

"Sleeping on the beach requires a permit." I made that up, but it sounds legit.

"Then I'll buy the house next to you."

"Which one?"

"Both."

I bark out a laugh. "You're serious?"

"*Nigdy nie byłem bardziej poważny, kochanie.* Never been more serious, baby."

I drink the glass of water, needing a moment to process. "I could eat. Could you eat?"

He smiles and kisses my cheek. "Sit. Let me feed you."

I take a seat at the breakfast bar and eye the kitchen. "I think I need coffee."

"Water will flush the alcohol out of your system faster, then you need sleep. Caffeine will only dehydrate you and keep you awake."

I quirk a brow. "See. Bossy."

Laughing he refills my water. "I speak the truth. But if you want coffee, I'll make a pot."

"Can you make eggs?"

"I can. I make a pretty good omelet or scrambled."

"You choose."

As he preps, he talks. "You threw me off from the first moment we met, as unconventional as it was. I wanted you—that was clear."

"For sex," I clarify.

"Yes and no." He sweats some onions on the stove as he cuts up ham and other veggies. "Like I said, you threw me off my game. I didn't know what to do with all I was feeling. The more I saw you, the more I liked you, the more I wanted. Not just for sex."

"But you offered—"

"*Idiota*, remember?"

"Go on."

"I offered what I knew I could handle. What I thought might not scare you off, but even then, I wanted more."

He did scare me off with that offer. "Your brother said something about a contract—"

"I'm getting there." Is he blushing? He throws everything in the pan with the onion to sauté. "Since I made my first million, I've found it hard to meet women who aren't looking for a sugar daddy or to be a trophy wife. Eventually, I stopped trying. I signed with an agency that would provide a service for what I needed. Discreetly, without complications."

"So you paid for—"

"Yes." He turns the stove down and stands before me. "I'm not proud of it, but it served its purpose. The day we met—"

"Holy! You thought I was one of your…"

"Yes." He squeezes my hand. "You have no idea how relieved I was that you weren't. I don't mix business and pleasure. But I also didn't want to know you were working at the agency, and I was just another client to you."

"And here I was thinking I was just another set of tits and ass."

"Never," he barks. His nose flaring, his shoulders rise and fall with each steady breath. "I never saw you as anything other than a woman to be worshipped—treasured."

My heart softens. "You called me a treasure the first time you saw me?"

"My heart knew you. It recognized who you were before I did." He presses his forehead to mine.

"And what's that?" My heart may have softened toward him, but that doesn't mean it's not pounding an erratic beat with nerves and excitement.

"My other half—My Queen. Moja Królowo."

"And your other women?"

He pulls back, stealing my gaze and my heart. "I haven't looked at or touched another woman since you walked into my penthouse all those weeks ago. I can't change my past, but I promise to give you all of my tomorrows if you'll just give us a chance."

The sincerity in his eyes and the conviction in his tone is enough to have me jumping to my feet and practically tackling him. "I thought you didn't date—"

"I'm only interested in dating you—"

"You don't do relationships—"

"There are only three relationships I want with you—well, maybe four."

"Four?!" What in the world is he talking about?

He holds up his hand, counting off. "Girlfriend first. Then wife. Eventually the mother of my children. And if you can stand to put up with me both day and night, client."

Four. That's four relationships he's willing to tackle—with me.

I thought I didn't mean anything to him.

I was nothing special.

Just another set of tits and ass.

Turns out he saw something special in me all along, just as I did in him.

It killed me that he only considered himself worthy of a sexual relationship when I saw so much more.

We were in the same boat. Neither of us saw ourselves as the other did. We thought we were lacking.

Yet we are perfect for each other.

"How do you say *yes* in Polish?"

"*Tak.*" He pulls me close, gripping my hips, a smile tugging at his lips.

"And how to you say—"

"*Kocham cię.*" He presses his mouth to mine for a soft, tender kiss. "I love you. *Kocham cię.*"

He loves me. My eyes prick with happy tears. "*Kocham cię,*" I fumble.

"Again," he breaths across my lips.

"*Kocham cię.*"

"Now English."

"I love you, Dmitri. You better not break my heart," I warn. I've cried enough tears to last a lifetime.

"Your brother said he'd bury me six feet under if I did." His eyes light with humor.

"That's more a Scarlet thing." I laugh.

He joins me. "That's what I said."

Wrapping me in his arms, he grips the back of my neck, sobering. "Not letting you go, My Beautiful Treasure." Another press of our mouths. This time not so gentle and way more demanding. "I love you," he breathes into our kiss, into my life, into my soul.

"*Kocham cię*," I whisper, hoping I don't mess it up.

"*Kocham cię*, Mój Piękny Skarbie. I love you, my beautiful treasure."

THE END

Can't get enough?
Want to know what's next for Dmitri and Casandra?
Keep reading for their **Epilogue** and a chance to get exclusive
BONUS SCENES for newsletter subscribers.

Not ready to leave the Storm World? Check out Stefan's
story in Wicked Storm at dmckdavis.com/all-books/series/
stormbrothers/wicked-storm
Billionaire bad boy Stefan Storm has lived his life
in his brother's shadow.
He gambles, drinks, and chases women like it's a
sport—a game.
Wicked, dirty diversions are his forte until an
innocent stumbles into a game she doesn't
understand and has no hope of winning.
Will she make him see how deep he's fallen? Can he save her,
and possibly himself, before it's too late?

Are you a fan of alphaholes and sports romances?
Meet the men of my *Black Ops MMA* Series at dmckdavis.
com/all-books/series/black-ops-mma-series. They're
tough, determined, and sometimes too alpha for their own
good. NO MERCY at dmckdavis.com/all-books/series/
black-ops-mma-series/nm is Book 1 in the series. Gabriel
"No Mercy" Stone fell hard for his best friend's woman. To
hide his feelings, he ignored her and treated her like dirt.
But when things go south with her boyfriend, Gabriel is
there to pick up the pieces.
When it comes to protecting his Angel, he has no mercy.

Are best friend's sister, friends to lovers, and second chances more your style?
Then check out my Until You series at dmckdavis.com/all-books/series/until-you. Book 1, Until You Set Me Free at dmckdavis.com/all-books/series/until-you/until-you-set-me-free, is a heart-wrenching romance about a millionaire in the making and his best friend's younger sister. Joseph is everything Samantha is afraid to want, yet she's never wanted to be noticed so badly in her life. Samantha shouldn't even be on Joseph's radar, and yet she is from the day she walks in the room, making him want what's not his to take.
Some loves are just destined to be,
regardless of how hard you fight it.

Are First Responders your jam?
Then let me introduce you to Reid and his Daisy. WILDFLOWER is a heartwarming, secret crush, first responder, steamy contemporary romance between a firefighter and a local flower shop owner.
She's a five-alarm fire he has no desire to extinguish.
Check out the *WILD* Duet today at dmckdavis.com/all-books/series/ashfordfamilyseries.

This is a dream for me to be able to share my love of writing with you. If you liked this book, please consider leaving a review on Amazon and/or on Goodreads.

Personal recommendations to your friends and loved ones are a great compliment too.
Please share, follow, join my newsletter at dmckdavis.com/subscribe, and help spread the word—let everyone know how much you love Dmitri and Casandra.

EPILOGUE

TWO THINGS HAPPEN THE SECOND WE STEP inside Casandra's beach house after spending hours swimming and playing on the beach.

One, the house smells like home, and I don't mean Vegas. I mean, New York, *living above my parents' bakery* home. Fresh-baked bread, onions, and meat assault my senses. I groan in satisfaction, my mouth watering as my stomach rumbles, reminding me it's way past lunchtime.

Two, the voices coming from the kitchen confirm we've got company—company that cooks.

Grabbing my girl's hand, I practically drag her to the kitchen to meet my sister. Nerves prickle under my skin. The two most important women in my life are getting ready to meet.

"Mina." I entwine my arms around Cas' waist, holding her against me as we face my sister. "This is Mój Piękny Skarbie, Casandra."

Mina squeals and rushes us. "I'm so happy to meet you!" She pulls my girl out of my arms and into a hug, whispering, "Has he told you what that means?"

"My treasure?" Cas glances at me over her shoulder for reassurance."

"My *Beautiful* Treasure," Mina and I harmonize as I pull Cas into my arms.

Mina squeezes Cas' hand. "Isn't that the sweetest love name?"

Zeke gives me a smirking chin nod over Mina's head. "Boss. Casandra."

Cas practically hides in my chest in embarrassment at seeing Zeke again before finding her voice. "It's nice to meet you, Mina. Good to see you again, Zeke."

I'm hoping she'll get over her mortification of Zeke possibly seeing us in the middle of having some of the hottest sex of my life. I can't say *the* hottest, as each time with My Treasure just gets better and better.

"Your brother and sister just got here. They're getting settled," Zeke informs Cas before giving me a loaded look, letting me know we need to talk.

I raise a brow, asking if it's urgent, and he gives me a barely perceivable negative head shake. Important but not urgent.

"How long before we eat?" I lace my hand with Cas', ready to pull her away to clean up.

"Probably an hour," Mina advises, already lost in checking on the food.

Perfect. "We'll be back."

"We can't just leave them," My Treasure whispers as we near the hall to our room.

"They're adults. They'll be fine." I pick her up and nuzzle her neck, making her squeal. "Besides, I need a minute with you before we have an evening of family."

"Really?" Her doe-eyed gaze has me hard in seconds. She's insecure about how much I want her—need her.

"Always." I set her on her feet in our ensuite bathroom and turn on the shower. As I strip out of my swimsuit, she watches me instead of joining me. "Need you naked, baby."

I've loved on her for the last twenty-four hours. We're still so new, working through the emotions of her hurt and my overwhelming desire to give her whatever she needs.

I'd given up on love.

Now, every dark, empty, lonely cell in my body has been filled with love for her. Here she is—my love—slipping off her suit, showing me her heart in every gesture and vulnerable moment. I can't get enough. I don't want to leave the bubble we've created here. Which is why we're staying the week.

We both need more clothes and our laptops that, in her haste to run and mine to find her, we forgot. So, our families brought what we needed. It's a great excuse for a little downtime with family, giving them a chance to get to know each other and us. They'll stay a few days and then head home since we have businesses, and they're key to keeping the wheels moving. A few days for family won't kill any of us, unless, of course, if Stefan were here. Then death would be a possibility if he said a cross word to Cas.

It's too soon to invite him into our bubble. He and I need to have words, and I'm not subjecting her to him while she's still getting used to the new status of our relationship.

Relationship. The word doesn't even make me break out into a sweat. It *does* make my cock hard and my heart light.

My parents would have loved Cas. "How do you feel about Christmas in New York? I'd like to show you my parents' bakery, where I grew up." The city is spectacular at Christmas time.

"But that's months away."

I step closer. She doesn't get it. "I'm not going anywhere, baby. I'm all in. Make plans with me."

Her face lights up under the spray of water as she rinses her hair. "And New Year's?"

That's my girl. Believe in us. "Absolutely." Whatever she wants.

"It sounds amazing. Maybe it'll snow. I've never had a white Christmas."

I'll make sure she sees snow for the holidays even if I have to truck it in. "It will."

Sand, sun, and ocean washed off, I grip her ass and garner her mouth with the need to get a little dirty. Backing her against the wall, I devour her like I haven't kissed her in weeks, when we spent most of the day making out in the ocean. She's had me worked up for hours.

She gasps across my lips, breaking our kiss when I slip two fingers inside her.

I growl and harden further with her soft heat enveloping my digits. "So fucking wet for me, Mój Piękny Skarbie." I fight the urge to stuff her full of my cock before she's ready.

With ravenous kisses and her body begging me to give her more, I drop to my knees.

"Dima." Uncertainty swims in her eyes.

Love her calling me Dima. It's new and does something crazy to my heart. "It's been too long since I've had your taste on my tongue."

"You just kissed me." She runs her fingers through my wet hair, gripping it. She's not really objecting.

"And I intend to kiss you again," I lift her leg over my shoulder, running my nose along her pussy lips, ready to feast, "—right here."

My groan as the first taste of heaven blocks out my girl's plea. The need in the pitch of her hips and her grip in my hair conveys all I need to know: she loves my mouth on her. No matter how shy she may be at first, a few licks and she's all in, giving herself over completely.

I'm starved. Famished. As if I haven't tasted her before. As if I've never known the joy, the hunger of pleasing a woman this way. Her leg nearly gives out when I kneed her insides—one finger and then two. The perfect amount to maneuver, teasing her G-spot, drawing elongated moans and mumbled praise from her precious mouth.

How I ever thought I only wanted a sexual relationship with this woman is beyond me. I was an *idiota*. From our first kiss to now, she unearthed a cavernous void in my life, in my soul, I knew was missing. I'd grown accustomed to ignoring it. I hid it so well. I really thought I didn't need love. That fully vetted sexual encounters would be enough to sustain me indefinitely.

I was an *idiota*. Clearly.

Now, on the other side, the chasm overflowing with her love and mine, it's plain to see I was only fooling myself.

Mina saw it—my capacity to love.

Casandra unleashed it.

Unleashed.

Unleashed.

Unleashed.

"Please, I…" My love's words are lost on a cry as she comes undone, tumbling over the edge, gripping my shoulder and head to stay upright, quivering, quaking.

Sucking and licking, I eat up her release, savoring her essence, feeling marked by her. Claimed and remade.

I turn off the water, dry us off, and carry her to bed.

Without missing a beat, she flips over on her tummy, raising her ass in offering. I settle in behind her, pushing my cock through her swollen, glistening pussy lips, gripping her ass. "Is this what you want? Me taking you from behind, *Moja Królowo*?"

"Yes," she pants, looking over her shoulder, biting her lip.

She starts to rise, but I stop her with a hand on her back. "Head down." It's a better angle for hitting her sweet spots. Plus, I can really drill into her without knocking her off balance.

Without warning, I slam inside, filling her to the hilt. To be inside her again, takes my breath. "*Taka piękna cipka. I to wszystko jest moje,*" I growl, shoving through her clamping muscles over and over.

The sounds of our joining—the slap of skin on skin and plunging through her wetness—fills the room, along with her gasps and my groans with each thrust.

Faster and faster.

I grip her hips.

Pound.

Pound.

Pound.

"More," she cries as her legs shake. She's nearly there. "Talk dirty to me in Polish."

I freeze for half a second, believing her *more* meant harder thrusts, but my girl wants my words.

I'll never deny her anything.

Through powerful thrusts, I release my native tongue. Dirtiness that would make her blush wrapped in loving sentiments that feed my soul rain down on her.

Blanketed in sweaty dew and labored breaths, she falls over the edge, gripping the sheets and calling my name.

I hold off a few more pumps before she's dragging me after. Falling, falling, falling without regret but with promises to love her gently before the night is over.

"Mój Skarbie." I kiss up her back, making her shiver and quake around my cock. I groan and shove in deeper, tiny tremors forcing the last of my seed inside her.

Dinner is amazing. Some of the best food I've ever tasted. Roasted meats with succulent vegetables, fresh salad with homemade dressing, hot buttered rolls, and a salted-caramel cheesecake. "I think I've died and gone to heaven."

"Naw, it's just Mina and her heavenly food. It's easy to confuse the two." Zeke swallows the last of his wine, missing Mina's blush and quickly hidden surprise over his doting compliment.

His eyes rarely left her all evening, jumping up to fetch whatever she needed or missed in laying out the food. Dmitri is deep in conversation with Gavin, so I'm not sure he's noticed, but I think Zeke has a thing for Mina. And my dear sister Scarlet has been eyeing Zeke like she just found a new chew toy.

I kick her foot, garnering her eyes. "No," I mouth, accentuating with a stern furrow of my brow before anyone notices.

She rolls her eyes and grabs another roll. "I'm going to gain ten pounds this weekend." If she can't sex her way through the weekend, she's going to eat her way through it.

I squeeze Dmitri's thigh, hoping I might have a lot of both. He does a double take when his gaze catches on my mouth as my hand drifts upward to grip his cock through his jeans. He stills my hand, bringing it to his lips for a tender kiss before placing it back over his lap, giving me a heated wink.

Yes, there's definitely more sex on the table tonight. But coffee and another slice of cheesecake are in order. A girl needs her sugar and caffeine to fuel the late-night escapes I'm hoping for.

"Where will you live?" Mina asks from the other end of the table, drawing all eyes to me, then to Dmitri and back.

Blood rushes to my ears, not wanting to give the wrong answer. We haven't discussed it. I figured he'd keep his place, and I'd keep mine. I mean, we just got together.

"Wherever she likes," Dmitri answers, his eyes on me seconds before he urges me out of my chair and onto his lap, kissing my neck. "Wherever she's happy." His fingers sink into my hair, pulling me closer so his words are private, whispered across my lips, "But wherever you are, I'm there, Mój Skarbie. Not letting you go."

My heart pounds for a whole other reason when he seals his declaration with a kiss that curls my toes and soaks my panties.

He breaks our kiss, pulling way enough to lock eyes. "Do you have a problem with that, Cas?" His voice is so gentle, it's a soft caress over my cheek.

The hope in his eyes helps me settle on an answer that surprises me but feels right. "I want to be where you are."

He nods, hugging me close. "*Dobra dziewczynka.* Good girl," he whispers.

I stand and hold out my hand. "Take a walk with me."

He doesn't hesitate in taking my hand. Standing, he addresses the room, "We'll be back."

We don't make it far, just out of the reach of the porch light before he draws me close. "Are you sure about what you said in there? I don't want you to feel pressured into agreeing because we had an audience."

I take his hand, pulling him along to the side of the house to the gazebo that came with the property. On one side is a hammock, on the other is a porch swing, and a table and chairs fill the space between. Near the hammock, I reach under my sundress and pull off my panties.

"What are you doing?" His gaze darts around to be sure we're hidden from prying eyes before he grabs my panties and stuffs them into his pocket.

"I'm showing you my version of a *yes, I'm sure.*" I lift my dress to just below my ass and lie in the hammock. He quickly catches on and helps me steady it while I get situated on my back, knees up, ready to lift my legs so he can join me.

His brow pops. "How do you envision this working?"

"It'll probably be easier if you remove your jeans. Then you're going to straddle the hammock facing me and, well…"

"Unbutton your dress," he commands.

As he removes his shirt and jeans, I unbutton the bodice of my dress and slip my arms out of the straps, keeping the fabric over my breasts. He stands before me, his hard cock peeking out of the top of his boxer briefs.

"Have you done this before?" He frowns and I smile.

"No, but I've thought about it," I admit, glad it's dark and he can't see my blush.

"Really?" He straddles the hammock, leaving his feet on the floor, and pulls me till I'm flush against him with my legs over his. He leans forward, his heated gaze caressing my bare pussy to my covered breasts. One hand grips my waist and the other, the hammock above my head. "And who starred in this fantasy with you, Moja Królowo? My Queen."

I shiver at his endearment, pulling him closer. "No one in particular." I swivel my hips, his hard-on rubbing against me. "Are you up for it?" I'm going for teasing and confident, but I fear I've missed the mark.

He captures my mouth in a sweet kiss with a little tongue and a bottom lip suck before he pulls back, running his finger-tips along my cheek and down my neck to the fabric covering my breasts. "I'm up for anything with you." His eyes follow the movement before popping back to mine. "You need to be quiet, baby. Zeke will keep everyone in the house, but we don't know who might be out here roaming the beach."

It's a private beach, but still… My pulse picks up. "Should we—"

"No." He slides his hands under my open dress and squeezes my breasts, toying with my nipples, making me arch into his touch. "You're safe. No one will see us." He bends, sucking a nipple in his mouth as he unbuttons the rest of my dress. "Your pleasure is only for my eyes. *Moja*. Mine."

I fist the back of his hair, murmuring, "Yes, yours," as I lose myself in his touch, arching off the hammock when he dips his fingers inside and out, spreading my arousal to my clit before he circles it torturously. I clench around nothing and bite back a moan.

He pops off my nipple with a, "*Dobra dziewczynka.* Good girl," before moving to my other breast.

"Need you inside me," I plead.

"After you come."

"I want to come with you."

"You will."

There's no use in arguing. If I've learned anything, it's that he enjoys my pleasure nearly as much as I do.

"Dima," I moan when he slips his fingers inside me, pumping, hitting that spot that makes me see stars.

"So perfect. So mine," he breathes across my lips.

"You're mine too. Don't forget that." I tease his stubbly jawline with my nails.

"Never forget, baby. Never." He grazes my mouth with his. "Now I need you to come."

He sounds as desperate as I am to have his cock buried inside me. "Kiss me."

"Yes, my love." His growled words send a shiver down my spine and ramp up my impending orgasm.

I ride his hand as he fucks my mouth with this tongue in rhythm with his fingers. His heavy breathing and grunts turn me on so much, I clutch his shoulders, trying to pull him closer, hoping he'll finally give me what I want—what I need—him.

On a commanded "Come," the tingling starts in my toes, flexing and arching up my body, around my belly and spreading outwards. A ringing bliss pops and sizzles before exploding in wave after wave of electrified orgasm that barely starts to wane before he thrusts his cock inside me, covering my body with his.

Pressing me into the hammock, he swivels his hips. His hold

on the netting above my head and his feet on the floor give him leverage to make every thrusting grind deep, packing a punch of utter pleasure.

"You feel so good, baby." His tender gaze locks on mine. "I won't last long. What do you need?"

"Just keep rocking against me." I'm close.

"Maybe this," he breathes into a heated kiss, moving his hand between us to rub my clit as his muscular chest rubs against my breasts. I wish he had an extra mouth or hand for my breasts. We may topple if he lets go of the hammock.

With my feet behind him, I press down on the netting and lift my hips, finding that perfect angle, holding it, grinding into him as he does the same to me.

"Oh, f—" he growls into our kiss, stealing my words, breathing harder, thrusting deeper. Desperate. Needy. It's such a turn on to know I get him this hot. He's finding pleasure in my body, in my ecstasy—in my need for him.

When my orgasm hits, it's all-consuming, life-altering, blinding bliss. Shaking through his own release, he pins me down, keeping us on the hammock. Kissing me.

Kissing me.

Kissing me.

Until our lips are swollen and he's hard again.

"Come here, Moja Królowo." He disentangles from me on a groan. Standing, he pulls me off the hammock and over to the swing.

He sits down, his erect cock glistening from our lovemaking. He pulls me down to straddle his lap and slowly enters me an inch at a time. Pushing off the floor, we start to swing. I grip his shoulders, fearful of falling off.

"I've got you," he assures. His hand gripping my ass moves us into a slow circular grind. His other hand, between us, rubs my clit. "Slow, baby. I want to feel every tremor, every shockwave before, during, and after you come."

I circle his neck, kissing him slow and easy, relishing the fullness and the back and forth of the swing.

When my need rises, he doesn't let me quicken the pace. He forces me—in the best of ways—to feel everything he's giving me, every inch of his mouth, his tongue, his cock, his hands, his body pressed to mine. My dress flows behind me, tickling my skin as it takes flight and then settles against my back only to take flight again with each downswing.

I'm naked from the front. He's nearly naked with his boxer briefs down but still protecting his ass on the wood seat.

After he brings me to orgasm, he lifts me off. "Turn around and bend forward."

I do as instructed, thankful to stretch my legs and save my knees from the hard surface with no give.

He fists my dress. "Widen your stance."

I do.

Gripping my hips, he pulls me down, my legs on either side of his, his cock right at my entrance. "Sit down, baby."

Hands on his knees, I lower myself till he's balls-deep and my ass hits his lap.

"Fuck. Your wet pussy is pure heaven."

I shudder, nipples hardening, then lean back. His hands cup my breasts, and his mouth finds my neck. He pulls and twists my nipples, fueling the movement of my hips.

"You're going to come just like this." He fingers my clit then runs his hand lower, rubbing the spot right before my opening where his cock is stuffing me full. "Then I'm going to bend you over the rail and fuck you hard till we both come again. Then shower. Then bed."

"Sounds like heaven," I pant against his jaw as I turn to kiss and nip it.

Bare to the world, my love does exactly as promised, except it's a bath we take instead of a shower. I'm not complaining one bit.

He loves on me throughout the night, making me come so many times, it has to be a world record. Call Guinness World Records.

Sometime before dawn, we tumble into each other's arms, murmuring *I love yous* as we fall into an exhausted sleep.

I don't like waking up alone. I've grown attached to having my girl in my arms as I sleep and wake. The house is quiet despite the number of people staying here and the hour. It's late morning. I slept in but truly only slept a handful of hours after loving my girl all night mixed with catnaps here and there. I might be a walking zombie today, yet I have no regrets. Coffee is definitely called for.

My Treasure's soft giggle has me slowing before I'm seen. Not eavesdropping… more like appreciating her enjoying a quiet moment with whoever is in the kitchen with her.

"—you shouldn't be embarrassed. I didn't see anything. I know when to keep my gaze averted." Zeke's gruff voice is tinged with amusement. He likes Cas. He has since the first day he stopped her from leaving at the valet stand.

"You've probably been in that situation a lot." I smile as my girl digs for gossip.

"Not as much as you're thinking. Besides Mina and me, no one else has swum in his pool. Boss is private. He never took his… I mean, he didn't—"

Cas laughs. "It's okay. You don't need to elaborate. I know about his contract girls."

I come around the corner and kiss her shoulder. "There's no one but you, Moja Królowo."

"Dmitri." She leans into me. "Did we wake you?"

"No, my love, my stomach did." I sit at the breakfast bar beside her. "Thanks." I take the proffered cup of coffee from Zeke, doctoring it with cream and sugar. "You been up long?"

"Long enough to grill me about you," Zeke teases, a rare smile tipping his lips.

"Hey! You brought it up. Not me." She blushes.

No, my girl wouldn't have mentioned Zeke seeing us having sex in the pool. Zeke is an intuitive guy. He noticed her bout of shyness whenever he neared. He likes peace. If he couldn't figure out why, he would have asked. I'm glad he cleared the air.

"You sorted?" I kiss her cheek, the scent of her filling my nose reminding me of all the sex we've had. She's got to be sore. Maybe a lazy day on the beach is what we need.

Zeke sets plates before us full of egg casserole, potato hash, and biscuits. "You eat?" I ask as he leans against the counter sipping from his mug.

"Yeah. I helped Mina prep and ate with her before they left."

"Where'd they go?" Cas asks before taking a moaning bite of eggs.

"Shopping for surf and turf fixings. I told her I'd grill if she'd do everything else. We're thinking a day on the beach before we head home tomorrow."

"Sounds good." I eye my girl's light skin. "You have sunscreen, right?"

She bumps my shoulder. "Of course. It's not my first day in the sun. Everyone needs to wear it, not just me. Oh, there are some lounge chairs and shade thingies we can put out too. Make a whole day of it. There's a cooler here somewhere. Maybe they can get ice on their way back?"

"On it." Zeke pulls out his phone, walking out of the kitchen. "Hey, Mina—" he trails off.

"You okay, Cas?"

Her eyes pop wide before settling into a frown. "Yeah, why wouldn't I be?"

I shrug, buttering her biscuit. "My sister and Zeke are important to me. I want you to feel comfortable around them."

"If you can put up with my sister, I can put up with the possibility of Zeke seeing us in a compromising position. Though I'd rather avoid it in the future."

What we have is only for us. "Noted." I hold up half the biscuit for her to bite. She does and groans her approval.

My cock twitches, getting ideas. "Do you maybe have a swimsuit that's like a turtleneck with boardshorts or something?"

She giggles. "No. Why?"

"My goal is to keep my hands off you today. Give you time to—"

"Heal?"

"—I was going to say recover. But, yes, heal works too. You okay? I've been a little hard on you."

"You've been entirely sweet—"

"Sweet?!"

"—and loving—"

"I'll take loving."

"—and tender."

I kiss her nose. Her lips. Fist the back of her hair and drag her closer. "You keep sweet-talking me—"

"You'll bend me over this counter."

"Counter, couch, dining room table—"

"Maybe tomorrow when it's just the two of us."

"It's a date."

My girl's smile is pure, radiant happiness. "I can't wait."

"About that turtleneck—"

"I do have boardshorts and a swim shirt I could wear."

"*Could* wear?"

She shrugs. "I like knowing you want me."

"You could wear one of those huge bubble parkas, and you'll still be the sexiest woman alive."

She melts into me. "See, so damn sweet."

"Tall, dark, and sexy—"

"—Bossy. It was Mr. Tall Dark and Bossy, I believe."

"No, I think it was Sexy."

"Hmm," she shrugs, "are you wearing your swim trunks?"

"Yeah." I don't have anything else.

"You torture me too, you know. Hanging low on your hips, showing off your tight abs and tempting obliques. A girl could combust watching you all hot and wet from the ocean."

"You keep talking like that, and we won't make it out of our room—"

"Not complaining." She tips a shoulder before slipping out of her seat, pulling off her t-shirt to reveal a teeny-tiny royal blue bikini that barely covers her ass and supple breasts.

I groan and adjust my cock, which is growing in appreciation. "Skarbie," I warn.

She backs away toward the patio doors. "Maybe if we hurry, we can have sex in the ocean before everyone gets—" She shrieks as I lunge for her.

She barely makes it down the stairs before I'm on her, throwing her over my shoulder as I run for the ocean. It's a good thing I put on my swimsuit before I came out, otherwise, I'd be buried balls-deep in her on our bed.

Though I guess I've changed my mind about no sex day—*she's* changed my mind.

"My naughty Skarbie, who knew genius computer nerds were this sexy?"

"Who knew Polish-speaking billionaire casino owners were the hottest thing in town?"

I slap her ass, squeezing away the sting. "We're going to have a great life, you and me." My hand slips between her thighs, rubbing over her clit.

"Dmitri," she gasps.

"You keep teasing me, baby, and I'll keep making you come."

"Sounds like a sure thing."

"And I only bet on sure things." I slide her down my body at the edge of the lapping water. "*Kocham cię*, Mój Piękny Skarbie."

"I love you too, Dima."

She kisses me like I'm the best of all her tomorrows.

I kiss her like she's the best of everything.

The billionaire and the genius. We make quite a pair.

Who knows what the future holds? As long as I have my girl by my side, we're unstoppable.

She tugs at my t-shirt, forcing me to break our kiss to toss it behind me before picking her up, urging her to wrap her legs around my waist. "Now what was this about sex in the ocean?"

"I said you'd better hurry before we have company."

"Zeke will keep everyone at bay."

"I'm starting to love that man."

I growl, and she laughs. "He only has eyes for one girl, and it certainly isn't me."

"What?! Who?"

"Oh, lord, you don't…" She grinds her hips against me, forgoing whatever she was going to say.

It doesn't matter. I forget what we were talking about and start walking.

"Make me come," she breathes across my lips, gasping as cool water hits her ass.

"Bossy," I tease.

"Maybe I'm Mrs. Bossy Pants."

"You're Mrs. About To Get Fucked in The Ocean." I pull her bottoms to the side, slipping my fingers through her folds from behind.

"Seems a little wordy."

"I could just call you Mrs. Storm." My heart pounds. Will she freak out? Will she run?

"What?!" Her grip on me tightens as I work to free my cock.

"Marry me, Casandra Vaughn. Give me a brood of little genius babies that look just like you. Let me spend the rest of my life loving you."

"You're serious?" she whispers.

"*Nigdy nie byłem bardziej poważny, Kochanie.*" I enter her slowly, brushing my lips across hers. "I'm as serious as I am hard."

"That's really serious then." Her eyes fall shut for second as I sink in further.

I chuckle and flex my hips as I grip her ass and fill her to the brim. "I love you, Cas. I know we need time to get to know everything about each other. But you're it for me. Marry me next week or a year from now, I'm still loving you through each and every day. Why wait?"

"Why wait," she repeats. Not a question.

Don't tease. "Is that a *yes*?"

"I think it is."

"I need you to be sure, baby."

"Yes. It's a *yes*."

"*Dobra dziewczynka.*" I hold the back of her head and ass, drilling into her mouth and pussy. "*Moja.*"

"*Moja,*" she repeats.

"Every day of every minute, Moja Królowo."

BONUS SCENES

Want more Dmitri and Casandra?

Join my mailing list to receive exclusive BONUS Scenes for Dmitri and Casandra.
Bonus Scenes are only available for newsletter subscribers.

Get **BONUS SCENES** here:
https://BookHip.com/ZZNJDXL

ABOUT THE HOT VEGAS NIGHTS SERIES

I hope you enjoyed my book, *Vegas Storm*, which is part of the shared world Hot Vegas Nights.

Would you like to read all of them?
Find them on Kindle Unlimited.
www.subscribepage.com/hotvegasnights

The Vegas Strip is the gateway to your wildest fantasies. Where debauchery rules and depravity runs rampant. Elusive billionaires, celebrity bad boys, tantalizing dancers, master mixologists, and sexy tattoo artists are all within reach.

During these 15 Hot Vegas Nights, you'll take a
chance on love, lose yourself in entertainment,
and gamble your heart away!

Fifteen books all written with your pleasure in mind.

Vegas Baby by Melanie A. Smith

Vegas Prince by Mckenna James

Vegas Showdown by Amy Stephens

Healing in Vegas by Sydney Aaliyah Michelle

Vegas Reward by Michelle Donn

Playing Vegas by CL Collier

What Happens in Vegas by Sabrina Wagner

The Vegas Pitch by Amanda Shelley

Waking up Married in Vegas by Kaylee Monroe

A Vegas Dare by Kate Stacy

Vegas Valet by TL Mayhew

Vegas Redemption by Anise Storm

All's Fair in Love & Vegas by Shannon O'Connor & M Leigh Morhaime

Vegas Storm by D.M. Davis

Vegas Jackpot by E.M. Shue

ACKNOWLEDGMENTS

First and foremost, thank you to my heavenly Father for giving me a tender heart that always felt a little broken until I learned how to share it with the world through my stories.

Thank you to my family. You are my heart, my backbone, my little peace of heaven. I do this because of you.

To my Divas, thank you for taking a chance on me and my books and then sticking around for the silly stuff that goes on in my reader group. You make me laugh and give me more than you'll ever know.

To my editors, Tamara and Krista, thank you for reading my words, dressing them up, making them presentable for the world.

To Ashley, thank you for finding me, sticking with me, supporting me, listening to my breakdowns, and helping me climb back up. You are a light in a world of doubt.

To Anna, thank you for your generous heart in helping me with the Polish translations. Any errors are on my part for making changes without your review. Our hearts go out to you as you live through the devastation inundating your beloved country. Stay safe.

To the readers, thank you for picking up this book. I pray it won't be the last of mine you read. I do this hoping there's one person out there who finds joy, solace, understanding, and love in my words. We all deserve to be seen. I see you.

I'll keep writing. You keep reading, and don't forget to leave a review.

Until next time. Blessings, Dana

ABOUT THE AUTHOR

D.M. Davis is a Contemporary and New Adult Romance Author.

She is a Texas native, wife, and mother. Her background is Project Management, technical writing, and application development. D.M. has been a lifelong reader and wrote poetry in her early life, but has found her true passion in writing about love and the intricate relationships between men and women.

She writes of broken hearts and second chances, of dreamers looking for more than they have and daring to reach for it.

D.M. believes it is never too late to make a change in your own life, to become the person you always wanted to be, but were afraid you were not worth the effort.

You are worth it. Take a chance on you. You never know what's possible if you don't try. Believe in yourself as you believe in others, and see what life has to offer.

Please visit her website, dmckdavis.com, for more details, and keep in touch by signing up for her newsletter, and joining her on Facebook, Instagram, Twitter, and TikTok.

ADDITIONAL BOOKS BY
D.M. DAVIS

UNTIL YOU SERIES
Book 1—Until You Set Me Free
Book 2—Until You Are Mine
Book 3—Until You Say I Do
Book 3.5—Until You eBook Boxset
Book 4—Until You Believe
Book 5—Until You Forgive
Book 6—Until You Save Me

FINDING GRACE SERIES
Book 1—The Road to Redemption

BLACK OPS MMA SERIES
Book 1—No Mercy
Book 2—Rowdy
Book 3—Captain
Book 4—Cowboy
Book 5—Mustang

ASHFORD FAMILY SERIES
WILD Duet
Book 1—Wildflower
Book 2—Wildfire

STORM BROTHERS SERIES
Book 1—Vegas Storm
Book 2—Wicked Storm
(part of the Wicked Games Anthology)

STANDALONES
Warm Me Softly
Doctor Heartbreak

STALK ME

Visit www.dmckdavis.com for more details about my books.

Keep in touch by signing up for my Newsletter.
Connect on social media: Reader's Group, Facebook,
Instagram, Twitter, TikTok
Follow me: Book Bub, Goodreads